ABLAZE

SHENANDOAH SHADOWS NOVELLA 3

MELISSA F. MILLER

BROWN STREET BOOKS

Trent sat in sullen, seething silence. Beside him, Ryan Hayes, Assistant United States Attorney and all around good guy, drummed his fingertips on the steering wheel.

Ryan cleared his throat, "It's temporary."

Trent blew out a long, loud breath. "I know. I just ... Ryan, I'd rather stand and fight than run and hide."

"Dude, I know. I get that. But I'm not sure you fully comprehend the situation you're in." Ryan stopped at a red light and glanced over at him. "Do you?"

Trent got it. And he knew Ryan was right. But

that didn't mean he had to like it. Ryan kept his eyes on Trent's face, waiting for a response.

"I do. You've got the light."

Ryan took his foot off the brake and gave the car some gas. "So, you understand that the Commonwealth Attorney has called a press conference, where he plans to announce an indictment against you for the murder of Rear Admiral Sampson?"

"Which we both know I didn't commit."

"Sure, right, and nobody's a bigger believer in our system of justice than I am. Under ordinary circumstances, I'd tell you to hire a top-notch criminal lawyer and wipe the floor with the prosecution."

"But these aren't ordinary circumstances because the Department of Defense is leaning hard on the Virginia prosecutor to nail me to the wall. I'm still innocent. So?"

Ryan shook his head and turned onto a tree-lined cul-de-sac. "So, a friend who works in the Office of the Commonwealth Attorney tells me they plan to request no bail."

Trent shrugged. "And?"

Ryan pulled into a wide driveway and

brought the car to a stop. He turned to face Trent.

"And an informant who's currently a resident at the county jail said there's already a price on your head. They don't want to lock you up to stand trial. They want to lock you up to silence you. You know, permanently."

Trent's jaw fell, and he clamped it closed. "You didn't mention that part earlier."

"I was hoping not to have to. I thought you'd trust that I was looking out for your best interests. You know, I could lose my job for this."

Trent suddenly felt two inches tall. He met Ryan's eyes.

"Thank you for putting it on the line for me. I'm sorry I'm acting like a dickhead."

Ryan threw back his head and laughed. "Apology accepted. Now there's one other thing I didn't tell you. It's about your temporary digs."

Trent peered up at the red brick house with its white-columned portico and side-entry garage. "Looks like a standard-issue suburban home. Anonymous, blends in with the neighborhood. Seems like a good place to lie low. So what's the issue?"

Ryan passed his hand over his mouth, then said, "You'll be sharing it with someone else. Obviously, I couldn't requisition a team of U.S. Marshals and a neutral site in your name. Not with the murder indictment about to come down. So, I reached out to a team I trust to keep a secret." He nodded up at the house.

"So, what? Am I bunking with a mob boss? A terrorist turned cooperating witness? Who's the scumbag?"

"Olivia."

Trent stared at Ryan for what had to be a full minute. When he spoke, he couldn't hear his own words over the rush of blood in his ears.

"Olivia? As in, Olivia Santos?"

Ryan clasped him on the shoulder. "The one and only. C'mon, it'll be fine. You hounded me for weeks to tell you where I stashed her. Well, now you know."

Ryan exited the car and approached a tall, gray-haired, bespectacled man in jeans and a golf shirt who came loping around from the side of the house. Part of the team assigned to protect Olivia, no doubt.

Trent sat in the car, frozen, trying to make

sense of the news Ryan had dropped on him. Being charged with murder, having a hit out on him—these were circumstances that would leave most people reeling. But, as far as he was concerned, the real bombshell was Olivia.

Olivia, who'd given him a fleeting glimpse of salvation and happiness—of life itself—and then threw it all away to play the hero. Olivia, who'd exposed a dirty web of corrupt politicians and then vanished without so much as a goodbye. Olivia, who filled his dreams every night, but not his bed in the morning.

He forced himself to open the car door and trudge toward the house. His legs were lead weights, and his chest was an iron cage. He wanted to tell Ryan to call it off: he'd rather take his chances with a shiv-wielding cellmate in the county lockup than in a four-bedroom, center-hall Colonial with Olivia Santos.

O livia shifted the curtain back into place and hurried out of the living room, racing for the stairs and the safety of her bedroom. Deputy Marshal Nicole Reese stepped into her path.

"Aren't you gonna stick around and say hi to your new housemate?"

From the tilt of the deputy marshal's head and the half-smile that looked suspiciously like a smirk, Olivia had a feeling Ryan had filled in her protective detail about her history with Trent.

"Um, later. I'm kind of sleepy." She stretched out her arms and yawned exaggeratedly.

Nicole eyed her. "It's two-thirty in the afternoon."

"Oh. Then I think I'll go for a run. Get my blood pumping, you know?"

"That's a good idea. You should invite the new guy. Get to know him."

Olivia pulled a face. "You obviously know I know him. So whatever you want to say, spit it out."

She wouldn't call the deputy marshal a friend, not exactly. But she was the closest thing Olivia had to one in her current situation. And they'd been living together for over a month. So they shared an easy familiarity. Not like the stiff, formal Deputy Marshal Dane Michaels, who'd cracked one smile—if that—in the thirty-seven days they'd been together.

Nicole's face softened. "Look, Ryan said you were involved with Mann. I don't know the details obviously, but you're just going to make it worse for yourself if you act all awkward. It's not like either of you has a choice about being here. You might as well make it as stress-free as you can."

She sighed. Nicole was right. "I guess."

She turned and pasted a smile on her face, ignoring her pulse hammering against her throat like a trapped bird.

"Thatta' girl."

"Why's he here, anyway?"

Nicole side-eyed her. "Hayes didn't tell you?"

"He said Trent needed to disappear for a while, that it was a matter of life and death, and there was no place he could go. I figured Ryan was exaggerating so I wouldn't try to object."

"I don't think AUSA Hayes exaggerates. Like ever. Your boy's about to be charged with murder. The prosecuting attorney is going to ask for detention until trial. And word's gone out through the jailbird grapevine: There's a cool quarter mil for anybody who takes him out."

A shiver ran along Olivia's spine. Gooseflesh pimpled on her arms. "There's a contract out on him?"

"Yeah."

Someone wanted Trent dead badly enough to pay two hundred and fifty thousand dollars to make it happen? Her head spun. She'd sacrificed everything to protect him. She'd sacrificed the possibility of *them* being something. And it had all been for nothing.

Her smile cracked and faded. Her stomach dropped. Her throat closed. She'd accomplished nothing. She'd squandered her chance at happiness. And now Trent would hate her.

"Chin up, Santos," Nicole whispered as the door opened and Dane and Ryan walked into the house. Trent followed a half-step behind.

He strode into the house with his head bent, studying the floor like it held ancient secrets. When he raised his face and looked at her, her breath caught. His face was a stone mask, but his eyes flashed betrayal and hurt. In an instant, the pain vanished—so fast that she was sure she'd imagined it.

He turned his gaze toward Nicole and smiled.

"Hi. I'm Trent. You must be Deputy Marshal Reese."

She stepped forward and shook his hand. "Call me Nicole. And, uh, you know Olivia."

He nodded. "Olivia." His voice was flat.

She swallowed. "Trent."

He stared at her for a half-second, then turned to Dane and adjusted the bag slung over his shoulder. "Wanna show me where I'm bunking?"

As Dane led Trent upstairs, Ryan gave Olivia's hand a reassuring squeeze. "He'll thaw out. Just give him some time."

She nodded mutely.

Nicole raised an eyebrow. "He'd better. This house isn't that big."

Ryan shrugged. "Part of this is my fault. I ... didn't tell him you'd be here, Olivia."

Olivia blinked at him. "What? Ryan—"

"He's a mule. It took forever to convince him to let me hide him. I thought—look, if he'd know you'd be here, I was afraid he'd refuse to come."

"He hates me that much?" Her soft, shaky voice made her cringe.

Ryan shuffled his feet, then coughed. "Uh, I think you broke his heart, Liv."

A silence fell over the hallway. The low rumble of male voices drifted down from upstairs as Dane showed Trent around. Olivia gaped at Ryan, who threw the deputy marshal a helpless look.

Nicole shook her head. "Well, family-style dinners are about to get interesting."

2

The U.S. marshal lingered in the doorway, while Trent looked around the airy bedroom. It was a standard-issue suburban guest room with neutral paint, neutral bedding, neutral everything.

"Everything okay?" Dane asked.

"Fine." Trent didn't plan on being here long. The accommodations made no difference to him. He tossed his bag on the bed and walked over to the window. He turned the louvered blinds to peer out into the treelined backyard. He noted that he couldn't see the neighbors, which meant the neighbors couldn't see them. Good.

He glanced over his shoulder. Dane was still standing there, half in the room, half in the hall.

"Thanks, man." He tried to dismiss the agent without being a jerk about it.

"Oh, yeah, sure. You need anything you let me know. I was thinking I'd head over to the grocery store, maybe pick up some steaks. Sound good to you?"

Trent shrugged. "Sure." Did steaks ever *not* sound good?

"Good. It'll be good to have a little more testosterone in this place; getting tired of salads."

Dane laughed, and Trent furrowed his brow. He wasn't interested in playing caveman with this guy. If Dane had an issue with his female partner, Trent didn't want to hear about. If he thought griping about the women was a shortcut to male bonding, he was wrong. And if he was trying to ferret out how Trent felt about Olivia, he was going to be disappointed.

Trent stared at him, expressionless for a moment. "Salad goes well with steak. Balanced diet and all that jazz."

Dane finally took the hint and left. Trent methodically unpacked the handful of clothes he'd snatched up at random while Ryan had sat outside his place, car idling. He arranged them neatly in the drawers. He opened the closet, lined up his shoes on the floor, and hung his jacket. A decade of military discipline ensured that he unpacked quickly and efficiently. He removed the small, heavy portable gun safe from the bottom of his duffle and shoved it into the corner of the closet.

He was in the en suite bathroom arranging his razor and shaving cream on the shelf over the sink when he heard a quick rap on the bedroom door. He poked his head out and yelled, "Come in."

He figured it was Dane coming to get his opinion of baked potatoes versus lady food like quinoa. But instead, Olivia's heart-shaped face came into view.

"I'm going for a run. Care to join me?" Her voice was cool but friendly.

He stepped out of the bathroom still clutching his toothpaste and eyed her. "Running, huh? It's what you do best, I guess."

She winced and fixed him with those ocean blue eyes, so deep he was afraid he might drown in them. "That's not fair."

"Isn't it? I seem to remember you telling me

you'd wait for me to settle Carla's score. You made me believe you'd be there. And instead, you took off."

She closed her eyes for a long moment and pressed her lips into a firm, thin line. Her nostrils flared as she tamped down her temper. He leaned against the doorframe of the bathroom and watched her wrestle for control. When she opened her eyes, her expression was clear and neutral.

"I understand that you're hurt or angry or disappointed or all three. But, it's not like I took off because I wasn't ready to commit. When I realized Carla's murder and the Qīng Líng bribery scheme were connected, I took it to Ryan to protect you—to keep you out of it," she said in a careful, gentle voice.

He bit off a bitter laugh. "That's rich. How many times have you told me you didn't need my protection? What makes you think I need yours?"

Her face softened. "Trent, don't."

"No. Answer me. Did I ask you to take care of this for me?"

She sighed. "No, you didn't. I did it anyway. If you can't forgive me for that, then this temporary roommate situation is going to be awkward. But I don't regret what I did."

He clenched his jaw and stared at her. "You should," he finally gritted out.

"Well, I don't. Senator Townes' involvement changed everything. This thing is ugly, dirty, and has tentacles all over the place."

He shook his head, rejecting her explanation.

She went on before he could respond. "I *am* sorry you've got a target on your back. I heard they're trying to pin Sampson's death on you."

He ground his teeth a moment longer, staring hard at her, reminding himself that he was angry. It was a reminder he needed because her presence in the room was melting his righteous rage. After a long pause, he realized she was still waiting for an answer.

"Yeah. Ryan will get it sorted. There's just a complicating factor—that's why I need to lie low for a while."

"A complicating factor. Is that what you call having a contract out on your life?"

"Ryan told you?"

"No, Nicole Reese told me. Who do you think—?"

He cut her off. "I don't know. I'm not

concerned about it." The last thing he needed was for her to try to fix another problem that didn't need fixing.

She shrugged. "Like I said, I'm going for a run. If you want to come along, I'm leaving in five minutes. If you want to sit here and stew about how much you hate me, go right ahead." She turned to leave.

"Olivia."

She paused in the doorway and glanced over her shoulder. "Yeah?"

"I don't hate you. I very much don't hate you." His voice was thick with emotion, and his pulse pounded in his neck.

Her bow lips softened into a slow smile. "Glad to hear it."

She pulled the door most of the way closed, leaving it open just a crack. But maybe a crack was all they needed to close the distance between them.

As her footsteps receded down the hall, he returned to the bathroom to dump the now misshapen and hot toothpaste tube on the sink. He'd apparently squeezed it into a mess while talking to Olivia. He ran a hand through his hair and headed over to the closet to grab his running shoes and his handgun.

When he jogged down the steps he found Olivia and Nicole Reese stretching in the kitchen. The marshal looked up at the sound of his footsteps. She reached for a water bottle on the island and tossed it to him. "Glad you decided to come along."

He snagged the bottle out of the air. "Why?"

"Because I was going to have to make you."

"Make me?" He eyed her.

"Yeah, Dane decided to go to the grocery store. He left before I had the chance to tell him Olivia and I were leaving. Protocol is neither of you can be here alone, so either she was going to have to stay or you were going to have to come. And I don't know you well yet, but I know how stubborn *she* is. So, you were coming whether you wanted to or not." She tossed her head in Olivia's direction.

Olivia smiled innocently. "There's a park on the other side of the cul-de-sac. It has a lake and a paved path. It's pretty."

She headed for the door and he trailed her. The marshal set the security system and stepped out into the backyard behind them. "She neglected to mention the part about the steep hills."

Trent rolled his neck. "Lead the way."

3

Olivia focused on the slap of her shoes against the pavement, the warm spring breeze on her face, and the chirping birdsong of the warblers in the trees —anything and everything to distract her from the man at her side.

It wasn't working. She was ridiculously aware of him. Of his even breathing, his strong back and shoulders, his graceful stride. As they crested a hill, she slid her eyes to her right and studied his profile as he took in the wide blue lake. As if he felt her watching him, he turned toward her, and the sun lit the gold flecks in his hazel eyes. Mercy, he was gorgeous.

She tripped over her loose shoelace and flew forward.

He thrust out his arm and caught her, coming to a stop and pulling her toward him before she hit the ground. "Easy, tiger."

"Um, thanks. Lost my footing."

He released her waist and nodded. "The view's distracting. Breathtaking, but distracting."

The view—that was what distracted her. Sure.

"My shoe's untied," she answered lamely as she crouched to retie it, bending her head over her the laces to hide her heated face.

He glanced behind them at Nicole, who was about an eighth of a mile behind them, just now jogging up the hill. "Your marshal doesn't seem to be in tiptop shape."

"She's giving us some space on purpose, I think. Last week, she dusted me—and I ran a six-minute mile," she said to her shoe.

He waited until she stood up, then cocked his head and studied her face. "Do we need space?"

"I'd like to set things right between us. Come on, let's run and talk." She needed to say her piece, and it'd be easier to do while they were in motion.

"A six-minute mile, huh?" He grinned and sprinted ahead.

She muttered under her breath and poured on the speed to catch him. She pulled up alongside him and matched his pace.

"I didn't mean to hurt you."

"So you've said."

She searched for a way to explain as they rounded a corner. "I've always put the job first. And before you say I don't have a job anymore ... I have to see this thing with Senator Anglin and Qīng Líng through. You get that, right?"

He furrowed his brow. "Sure. Just like I need to see *my* thing through—Carla's murder, Lloyd Sampson's faked suicide, the Boko Haram connection. But that doesn't explain why you ghosted me."

"I told you. It's all connected. I know it is. And there's no reason for both of us to deal with the fallout. I already had a target on my back, so I'm the logical choice."

He pulled up short and grabbed her arm, just above her elbow. "Hang on."

She came to a stop and turned to face him. "Yes?"

He huffed, not out of exertion, but frustration. "First of all, your plan didn't work. I *also* have a target on my back, remember? And, more importantly, I thought we were in this thing *together*. But you took off on your own, wanted to handle it all by yourself. You're just like—"

He clamped his mouth shut. But she knew.

"Just like Carla?" she asked softly.

Pain blazed across his face. After a long moment, he said, "Aren't you?"

This was different.

Wasn't it?

As she struggled for the words to explain, the ground under her feet trembled. Instantly— before the thought *seek cover* formed completely —she was diving into the bushes alongside the path. Beside her, Trent's muscle memory kicked in at the same time, and he rolled across the lawn and landed next to her.

A tremendous blast filled the air, sending flocks of birds squawking as they rushed from the trees. Car alarms wailed and blared. And then all went still.

They lay in the shrubs, silent and listening for another detonation, as they slowed their racing hearts and caught their breath. Olivia pulled herself up onto her elbows and tilted her head.

"It came from the southeast, right?" she whispered.

He nodded. "From the neighborhood."

They waited another moment. No booms, no sirens. They stood cautiously, just as Nicole Reese came trucking up the hill at lightning speed.

"You two okay?" she shouted as she approached, her weapon drawn.

"Yeah, you?" Olivia smiled shakily to reassure her.

"Fine." She came to a stop beside them. "That sound like a bomb to you?"

Olivia turned to Trent. He was the one with experience in a war zone.

He nodded. "An incendiary device of some sort. I think it came from the cul-de-sac or one of the streets between here and there. Maybe someone's gas tank exploded?"

By unspoken agreement, they headed back down the hill at a quick jog. The marshal holstered her gun. When they reached the nadir, they saw the flames and plumes of black smoke rising from behind a copse of trees.

Olivia's pulse ticked back up a notch. "That's definitely the cul-de-sac."

Nicole fumbled for her cell phone and jabbed at her contacts list.

After a moment, she rattled off instructions. "Dane, call me when you get this. There's been a disturbance near the location. If you're still at the store, do not proceed to the house until I can assess the situation."

They crossed the soccer field and emerged onto the street that connected with the cul-de-sac. The acrid smell of fire filled Olivia's nose, and she covered her face with her sleeve. Dark smoke hung low in the sky. As they reached the cul-de-sac, ash fluttered down on them like snow.

The safe house was engulfed in red-orange flames; they shot out of the front windows and the roof. A cluster of neighbors gaped up at the destruction from the other side of the street. As she pushed up against a wall of invisible heat. Olivia stopped walking and stared at the burning house.

"The car's not there. Thank God, Dane didn't come back yet." Nicole's voice cracked with relief at the confirmation that her partner wasn't inside the structure.

Olivia shifted her gaze to Trent, who nodded almost imperceptibly.

She cleared her throat. "I think you're the only one with a phone, Nicole. You want to call 911?"

"I'm sure one of the gawkers already did that. I'm going to sweep the area. Whoever set that off might have tried to blend into the crowd. You two stay put." She gestured toward a low stone wall.

"Got it."

Olivia and Trent lowered themselves to the wall as the marshal raced toward the house. The second she was out of earshot, Olivia leaned toward Trent, "You don't think it's just luck that Dane Michaels *happened* to leave for the grocery store, do you?"

"Hell no," he whispered back. "It *is* lucky that you wanted to go for a run after he left, though."

She bit her lower lip and tried not to think about how close they'd come to blowing up. "As soon as he hears that message, he'll know we survived. Which means …"

"Which means we need to get out of here. Now."

She glanced toward Nicole, trying to decide.

The woman was solid, Olivia was sure of that. But she'd take some convincing to bring around to the position that her partner had sold them out. And she'd want to go through the proper channels, report the incident up her chain of command, loop in the Department of Justice, and obtain another so-called secure location. They didn't have that kind of time.

She nodded. "Okay. There's a metro stop two blocks over. Let's go."

They stood and backed toward the end of the street, keeping their eyes on the marshal until she approached the backyard of the still blazing house, her phone in her hand.

"Now!" Trent said.

They turned and ran as distant sirens drew nearer.

4

Trent trailed Olivia through the entrance to the metro station. They pressed themselves against the curved wall, out of the path of foot traffic, to catch their breath and plan their next moves. He studied the faces of the commuters streaming by—bored, harried, tired. Nobody showed any interest in a man and woman dressed in running clothes.

For now, his inner realist warned.

Olivia turned her head toward him. "Are you armed?"

"Of course. You?"

"Yeah." She patted her hip. "I'm registered to conceal carry in the District. Are you?"

"No. You want to go to D.C.?"

"I want to check something at the National Archives. Plus, we need to talk to Ryan. We can take the Orange Line, hit the archives, and then wait for him outside his building."

"You don't even know if he went back to the office. He could be in court. Or on his way back here. I'm sure Marshal Reese has called him by now."

Her nostrils flared. "Do you have a better idea?"

"I agree we need to get ahold of Ryan. But D.C. is crawling with feds, and the U.S. Marshals will be out in force looking for us."

"So, what do you want to do?"

"We can't contact Ryan directly, but we can go through an intermediary."

"Who? Not Jake. That'd be riskier than lurking outside Department of Justice Head-quarters. Whoever wants us dead will be watching Potomac."

Not us, me.

The house didn't blow up until after he showed up. Whoever they were, they were gunning for him, not her. He thought about saying it, but the truth was they were in this together now, like it or not.

"Not Jake," he agreed.

"And not Marielle or Omar," she continued.

"Right."

Having friends who work for the CIA and DEA sometimes came in handy. Being on the run from the government was not one of those times.

She threw up her hands in frustration. "Then, who, Trent? Am I forgetting somebody?"

"Two somebodies. We call your cousin and ask her to get in touch with Omar's sister."

"Chelsea? She's a river outfitter and outdoor guide. And she doesn't even know Leilah Khan."

"That's the point. Nobody would expect us to try to get a message to Ryan through those two. If they've done their research, they'll sit on Jake, Marielle, and Omar, but not Chelsea and Leilah. You call Chelsea and tell her what to say to Leilah. Leilah can talk to Ryan without arousing suspicion."

She caught her lip between her teeth. "I don't want to get Chelsea mixed up in this. Why don't we just reach out to Leilah directly?"

He spread his hands wide. "Look, we don't know how deep this thing goes. Two intermediaries is safer than one."

She nodded her reluctant agreement. "I guess you're right. I don't love it though."

"I don't love anything about any of this, Olivia," he told her, keeping the roughness out of his voice.

"Aside from your gun, what do you have on you?"

He turned out the pockets of his athletic pants. "Nothing. My wallet's in the room, and I didn't bring my cell phone for obvious reasons."

She nodded. "I have two hundred dollars in cash, but that's it. No identification, no phone."

"You brought two hundred dollars with you on a run?"

"I did."

"Why? Is that CIA SOP?"

She looked at him with a blank expression for a long, long time before shaking her head no. "No, it's Olivia Santos Standard Operating Procedure."

"That's good. We can buy a burner phone to call your cousin. But, it's a kind of a weird habit, don't you think?"

Her eyelashes fluttered and she gazed down at the interlocking red hexagonal tiles that made up the floor. When she lifted her chin, her eyes were defiant.

"Mateo had a habit of leaving me places in Mexico City. We'd be at an embassy party or out to dinner with other couples, and I'd look around and he'd be gone. The first time I found myself stranded with no car and no cash was also the last."

Hot anger pulsed through his body. He clenched his fist and suppressed a low growl. Olivia's ex-husband was lucky he was more than three thousand miles away. The mistreatment she'd endured—had been made to endure by the CIA—gnawed at him, demanding retribution.

She tilted her head to catch his eye as if she knew what he was thinking. "It's over, Trent."

"Where'd he go? When he'd leave you?"

She arched an eyebrow. "To visit one of his mistresses, I imagine. Seriously, it's in the past. I'm glad to be free of him."

He was about to vow to make the man pay anyway when she suddenly flung her arms around his neck and nuzzled his cheek. He stiffened and froze for a millisecond. Then his hands found the curve of her hips and settled there as if they were home. He pulled her closer and pressed her body against his. They fit like a tongue and a groove. Connected, completed.

She pressed her warm mouth against his ear. A soft moan built in his throat. Then she whispered, "We have company. At nine o'clock."

His growing desire flickered, then faded. He shifted his head and cut his eyes over her shoulder to the entrance. Four U.S. marshals ran through the lobby. Their feet tattooed a staccato rhythm against the tiles, and their blue windbreakers with 'U.S. Marshal' emblazoned across the back in highlighter yellow flapped behind them. They fanned out—two to the left and two to the right—and thundered past the embracing couple without giving them a second glance.

As the marshals jumped the turnstile, Trent shook off his embarrassment and grabbed Olivia by the wrist. "Come on."

He pulled her back through the glassed-in lobby and out onto the sidewalk. They raced around the corner to the station's parking lot. He scanned the wide, paved area until he spotted the bus shelter. He beelined toward it.

"You want to take the bus?" Olivia huffed alongside him.

"No. But there'll be taxis hanging around to take people to the airport."

"Taxis? How old *are* you?" she teased him.

"Har har. Not everyone uses those ride-sharing apps, you know. Especially if you don't want to be tracked."

"Hate to break it to you, but there's a record if you take a cab, too."

"Ah, but not if we take a jitney."

She furrowed her forehead. "Pardon?"

"A jitney—it's an unlicensed cab. Just a private car you can hire to take you to your destination. For cash."

That earned him an appreciative nod. "You think there'll be one around here?"

"Yeah, I do. That airport fare is steep."

Sure enough as they neared the bus stop, one row over from the line of official taxis and the cars sporting ride share placards, several late model sedans idled. Trent loped over to a gold Chrysler whose owner, a balding, olive-skinned guy with a pronounced gap between his front teeth, leaned against the hood. The trunk was popped and open for business.

"Hi, there."

Before answering, the man appraised Trent

for a moment, then slid his eyes over to Olivia. They lingered a beat too long for Trent's liking, but he kept his expression neutral. Olivia flashed the man a bright smile, which he returned.

Then he turned his attention back to Trent. "You need a lift somewhere?"

"We do."

"Not the airport?" The guy opened his hands as if pantomiming their lack of luggage.

"Not the airport. We're going a little further out than that. You know the bread factory in Shenandoah Falls?"

Olivia's cousin's outpost was somewhere on the outskirts of the small town. They could walk from there. No need for this guy to know their exact destination.

The driver rubbed a hand over his shiny pate. "Bordman's Biscuits and Breads? Sure. But that's a ways. It'll cost ya ..." he paused to perform some mental mathematics, then said, "Seventy-five bucks."

Trent turned to Olivia and jerked his head slightly. She unzipped the shallow pocket set in the back waistband of her running tights and removed two tightly folded bills. She unfolded them and handed one to the man.

"You can keep the change," she told him.

He removed a worn leather billfold from his jacket pocket, smoothed the creases out of the hundred-dollar bill, and then carefully placed it inside his wallet.

He slammed the trunk closed and opened the back passenger door to usher Olivia inside. "Your carriage, milady. My name's Arjun, by the way."

"Thanks, Arjun." She gave a little laugh and eased into the car, scooching across the seat to make room for Trent. He nodded at the guy and slid in next to her.

While Arjun walked around to the driver's seat, she leaned in close to Trent and whispered, "About the ... thing ... at the metro station. I'm sorry."

He shook his head, puzzled. "What thing?"

She pursed her lips. "Really? The passionate embrace? I don't want to have another misunderstanding."

He squinted at her. "Misunderstanding? I'm not trying to be dense, Olivia, but I have no idea what you're talking about."

"Remember how you kissed me in the alley

in Shenandoah Falls—after we left Padric's Public House?"

Did he remember? Was she joking?

"Uh, yeah. I remember."

She twisted her hands in her lap. "Well, you were very clear that it didn't mean anything—it was only a cover. And I wanted to let you know I know it didn't mean anything this time, either. That's all."

He opened his mouth to tell her he thought they were past all that just as the driver yanked open his door and deposited himself behind the wheel. "We'll talk about this later," he said instead.

He spent the two-and-a-half-hour ride half-listening to Olivia and Arjun chat about Arjun's family, baseball, and the recipe for perfect Rasgulla, the sweet spongy dessert dumplings. Trent interjected here and there, but his focus wasn't on the conversation or even the fact that someone was trying to kill him. Instead, he thought about the need he felt for Olivia. It was more than attraction, more than desire. It was pure need.

His efforts to tamp it down in the weeks since she'd vanished had been fruitless. Sure, he had plenty to occupy his mind during the day—work, his clients, helping Jake track down the rogue operator who'd sold him out in the first place, finding Rear Admiral Sampson's killer. But, at night, when he closed his eyes, the image seared inside his eyelids was Olivia's face. Her blue eyes, sparking with fire. Her lips, swollen and red from his kisses. The sweep of her cheekbones. In his sleep, his hands traced the memory of the swell of her breast, the curve of her hip. But each morning, he woke up alone in his cold bed.

He shifted on the seat next to her and willed Arjun to drive faster.

5

Olivia waved goodbye to Arjun as the gold sedan pulled out of the bread factory parking lot and merged into the flow of light traffic.

Once the car was out of sight, she turned to Trent. "We should take the rail trail that runs along the river. There's less of a chance of being seen, and if we *are* spotted, we'll look like any other pair of joggers and not .... What are we, fugitives?"

He shrugged. "Fugitives is probably a fair description. How far is it to your cousin's store?"

She chewed on her lip while she estimated. "Probably somewhere between four and five miles. It's fairly flat, though."

"Piece of cake. Lead the way."

She hurried around to the back of the lot and climbed the rusted metal fence. As she dropped down to the dirt path, Trent vaulted over the fence and landed beside her on silent feet. He was unfairly graceful for a man his size.

She cut between a pair of chestnut trees and led him down a steep, rocky embankment. "We'll pick up the rail trail right behind the factory's loading bay," she explained, pointing up toward the long, low-slung building. A moment later she thrashed through a cluster of thorny shrubs and emerged onto the trail. "Here we are."

She began to jog, and Trent fell into step beside her. "How'd you know about this trail?"

"When I used to spend summers up at the lake house, I ran this trail all the time. It goes right past the lake. Chelsea biked it all the way to North Carolina the summer between her freshman and sophomore years of college."

They ran in silence for a while, the only sound their feet pounding against the packed gravel and the birds chirping overhead.

"Chelsea will help us, won't she?"

Olivia considered the question. She and Chelsea had once been tight, more like sisters than cousins. Although they'd grown apart, that was a function of diverging careers, living in different countries, and Olivia being married to a control freak. After a moment, she nodded. Chelsea would come through for her.

She said, "I'm pretty sure. I guess if she won't, we can spend the other hundred dollars to buy a burner phone and call Leilah ourselves."

"If we have to." He paused for a beat. "About what you said—"

"Look, is that a heron?" She pointed to a long-legged bird fishing in the river.

He arched a brow at the obvious change of topic but nodded. "Looks like."

"He's unlikely to find many fish there. Maybe some water snakes," she prattled.

She'd hoped that he would forget his promise to talk about what had passed between them in the metro station. What was the point? Sure, they had to acknowledge the physical attraction between them—it was impossible to pretend it didn't exist, what with the way her skin heated at his touch and his eyes darkened with desire when he looked at her. But animal attraction aside, it was also abundantly clear that they were *not* meant to be together.

For one thing, they were too much alike. They both wanted to be the protector, the leader, the alpha. For another, they both had ghosts, old wounds that still dogged them. Memories of Carla Ricci and Mateo Flores kept wedging themselves between Trent and Olivia. And finally, they kept finding themselves in high-adrenaline situations.

She knew from her field training that that energy needed to go somewhere, and, often, it went in a sexual direction. For all she knew, if she'd met Trent at the grocery store, she might not have given him a second glance. Theirs was a doomed union, and one of convenience.

She had *almost* convinced herself, when Trent blurted, "You realize they want to kill me."

"Who wants to kill you?" She blinked at the whipsaw change of subject.

"I don't know. But you've been staying in that house for weeks. If Dane Michaels wanted to kill *you,* he probably had plenty of chances. But the house exploded after *I* showed up."

The tightness of his voice told her where he was headed. She stopped and faced him, jogging in place to keep her legs loose.

"If this is the part where you say we should

split up for my protection, just skip it. We have to see this thing through together. I was wrong to cut you out before, and I'm sorry. But this has gone on long enough. If we work together, we can put this to bed for good. So save it, okay?" She flashed a smile to soften the message.

His jaw clenched. A muscle in his cheek twitched. His eyes bore into hers. After a moment, he sighed. "Okay. We're in this together until the end no matter what."

"No matter what."

He dipped his head, as if he were leaning down to seal their deal with a kiss. On their own accord, her feet started moving, and she raced away.

"Come on, we're almost there," she called over her shoulder.

They sprinted the final quarter mile. As they wound around a bend in the river, Olivia slowed her pace, then stopped. She pointed to a log structure with a green roof. "That's Chelsea's store."

She led him up the hill to the parking lot behind the River Falls Outfitters. Olivia scanned the lot and spotted Chelsea's SUV.

"There's her Forester. She's here."

"Go in through the back door?" He gestured to a windowless metal door.

"I don't want to scare her. Let's just walk in through the front door like normal customers and act casual. I think it's our best play."

His doubtful expression made clear that he disagreed, but he nodded.

They strolled around to the front of the building. She pushed open the door, and a bell overhead tinkled to announce their entrance. Olivia stepped inside and swept her eyes over the rows of tents and sleeping bags to the right. To the left, kayaks, paddles, and inner tubes lined the wall. She weaved a path through the racks of weatherproof clothes and shelves of dehydrated foods and first aid kits to the back of the building. Trent followed on her heels. She found Chelsea squatting behind the counter, filling a display case with fire starters, bug spray, and sunscreen.

"Hey, Chelsea," she called so as not to startle her.

Chelsea lifted her head. Shock rippled across her face, and her green eyes widened. She popped up from behind the counter and tugged on her long braid, wrapping it around her fingers, a nervous tic she'd had since childhood.

"What are you doing here?"

"Hello to you, too."

Chelsea dropped her braid, raced around the counter, and grabbed Olivia by the arm. "Come with me," she ordered, gesturing for Trent to follow as she hustled Olivia into a small hallway.

They hurried to the end of the hallway, where Chelsea pushed Olivia inside a cramped office then reached out and dragged Trent inside as well. Finally, she slammed the door closed and locked it.

"What's wrong with you?" Olivia demanded

"What's wrong with *me*? You're the one whose face is all over the news. I'm not wanted for attempted murder, Liv—you are."

"What?"

Chelsea cut her eyes toward Trent. "And your friend's wanted for attempted murder *and* murder—of that Navy admiral or whatever."

"What are you talking about?"

Chelsea's hands danced through the air, punctuating her answer. "They're saying you two tried to kill a pair of U.S. marshals. They've got pictures of you up on all the channels, asking people to be on the lookout for you. They said you're armed and dangerous. Are you?"

Olivia threw Trent a look that said *I'll do the talking*. He stared back, stone-faced.

"Well, we're armed. I wouldn't say we're particularly dangerous ... unless we get cornered. We didn't try to kill—or actually kill—anyone. Neither of us did. This is all a misunderstanding." She smiled encouraging at her cousin.

"Must be a pretty big misunderstanding. There's a reward and everything."

Olivia's stomach plummeted to her knees. "Arjun," she breathed.

"I don't know, he seemed to like you. Maybe he won't turn us in." Trent spoke for the first time since they'd entered the store. His voice was even and unwavering.

"How much is the reward?" Olivia asked.

"A hundred thousand dollars."

Olivia laughed bitterly. "I don't think he liked me that much, Trent."

Trent's mask slipped and a shadow of worry passed over his face. "We shouldn't have come here."

He turned to Chelsea. "You don't want to get involved in this mess. We'll leave."

Chelsea jutted her chin forward. Her eyes glinted with strength. "Now, wait just a minute. My cousin's in serious trouble. I'm not about to let her twist in the wind. Tell me how I can help."

6

T rent's abdomen bounced down hard against the floor of the SUV's cargo hold as Chelsea jostled the vehicle over a bump. From his left, he heard a soft *'oof.'* He strained to make out Olivia's shape in the near-darkness. Little light penetrated the blanket that Chelsea had thrown over them. And the stacks of camping gear she'd piled around their bodies loomed on every side.

He turned and aimed his mouth where he thought Olivia's ear might be. "Are you okay?" He whispered.

"Yeah," she whispered back. "By the way, you're talking to my elbow."

He chuckled and inched forward. "Better?"

She turned, and her eyes shone in the dim light. "Much."

"Are you sure about this plan?" He probed her because he wasn't at all certain it was fair to let Chelsea help them as much as she was.

Olivia let out a long breath, ruffling the tendrils of hair that fell over her face. "Yes and no. I'm confident it'll work. Chelsea called this backcountry cabin 'remote.' That means it's *really* off the grid. She thinks the houses around the lake are too close together. You've been there. Our nearest neighbor is almost a mile away."

"So that's the yes. What's the no?"

"I hate involving her ... and Leilah. They're civilians, and if we do end up being charged with attempted murder—"

"And murder."

"—and murder, she ... or both of them ... could be charged with aiding and abetting. Accessory after the fact? I don't know, bad stuff."

He scrubbed his hands over his face. "I know. Believe me, I know."

"Plus, I don't know how I'm going to access the records I want from some cabin deep in the forest."

"What records? The files you wanted to look for at the Archives?"

"Yeah."

"Like what? The Declaration of Independence? The Constitution? The Bill of Rights?"

He felt, more than saw, her roll her eyes. "No, Trent. I'm not concerned with the founding documents. NARA also provides a free link to CREST. And I figured accessing it from there would make the searches more or less anonymous."

He searched his memory of bureaucratic alphabet soup. "NARA is the National Archives and Records Administration, but I'm drawing a blank on CREST, unless you mean the toothpaste, which I doubt."

"CREST is the CIA Records Search Tool."

"Wouldn't that be CRST?"

She jabbed him in the ribs with her elbow. "Don't be a pedant. It's a searchable database of declassified documents."

"You're a brute, you know that? Anyway, what good are declassified CIA records? They've probably been sanitized and redacted to the point of being worthless."

"I know. But I can't get my hands on the good stuff. Not without involving Marielle, and—"

"And that's out of the question," he finished firmly.

"Right. So, the cleaned-up-for-public-consumption versions will have to do."

"What records do you want to see?"

"Embassy records for Abuja and Beijing."

His heart thumped. "You're looking into Jillian Martin. Carla's friend."

"And Senator Townes' niece. Not to mention Craig Martin's sister. I think … well, I'm not sure what I think, but I want to follow a hunch."

The SUV banked right as the terrain changed from bumpy road to off-road and Olivia rolled with it. She crashed into Trent and threw out an arm to steady herself.

"Sorry," she breathed.

He shifted onto his side to face her, and the SUV went airborne. He placed a hand on her hip to keep her from flying into the tower of camping gear. The blanket rose above them for a moment, billowing up like a parachute, and he glimpsed her face. Her lips, parted. Her eyes, glittering. He swallowed hard and stayed perfectly still, forcing himself not to move toward her. The vehicle vibrated and juddered beneath them, and Olivia braced herself with one hand against his bicep and the other against the side of the cargo hold.

The words tumbled out before he could stop them. "It did mean something when we kissed. You know that, right? Even though it *shouldn't* have—you were married, you were a client, we were on the run from multiple federal agencies and CNI agents—all excellent reasons why that kiss *couldn't* mean anything. But it did. It meant everything."

She exhaled a small, breathy *'oh.'* Then the tip of her tongue darted out to wet her lips. She inched closer, so close he could feel the heat rising off her body like a wave. She released her grip on his arm and wove her fingers into the hair at the nape of his neck and tugged him toward her.

He came willingly, his mouth already searching for hers. As he lowered his lips and she arched up to meet him, the Forester came to an abrupt stop. He lurched forward, banging his forehead on a lantern while a tightly wrapped sleeping bag fell off a stack and bounced off Olivia's face.

"We're here," Chelsea announced.

Trent groaned.

~

Chelsea whirled around the interior of the tiny, tidy cabin, opening windows to air it out, running the taps until the water ran clear, and, to Olivia's immense relief, flushing the toilet.

"Oh, happy day, there's indoor plumbing," she rejoiced.

Chelsea flashed her a grin. "Hot and cold. There's a gravity-fed, solar-heated rain barrel system on the roof. I wouldn't take a long shower, but you've got the basics covered. No electricity, though."

Trent clomped in through the open door, his arms laden with gear from the SUV. "This is the last of it."

"I threw in a bunch of fire starters, and there's plenty of dried wood out back. You can make a cooking fire in the firepit. There's a grill cover for it in the closet. As for warmth after the sun goes down, your best bet is gonna be body heat." She gestured to Trent and waggled her eyebrows.

"Good Lord, Chelsea." Olivia shook her head but couldn't suppress a giggle.

"Are you sure a fire's a good idea?" Trent frowned, all business.

Chelsea bobbed her head, and her tight braid bounced off her back. "There's nobody around to see the smoke. The closest campsite is a remote, rarely used backcountry site about five miles away on the other side of the falls and a river. It's a strenuous two-day hike in, and the trail isn't well-marked. Only the hard-core campers use it, and it's early in the season for them. One good rain and the river crossing will be chest high. You're good. I promise."

Olivia crossed the room and locked eyes with her cousin. "I owe you."

"Big time," Chelsea agreed.

She checked the time on her chunky black watch. "I better get back to civilization so I can call Leilah Khan before it gets any later."

"You're sure you know what to say?"

"I'm sure. You need her to let Ryan Hayes know that the explosion was an inside job by the U.S. Marshal Service."

Olivia pulled her cousin into a tight hug. "Thank you."

Chelsea squeezed her back then held her at arm's length. "You'd do the same for me. We're family. I'll be back tomorrow afternoon, if I can. Otherwise, the next morning, okay? Just sit tight." Her eyes swept over Trent. "Don't do anything I wouldn't do."

Trent smiled at her. "Really, thanks for everything."

She surveyed the room one last time, then pulled her sunglasses out of her backpack and headed for the door.

"Hey, wait. Do you have any paper on you? And a pen?" Olivia asked.

Chelsea tented her eyebrows and thought for a moment, then dug a small traveler's journal and a graphite pencil out of the side pocket of her bag. "Here you go."

"Thanks."

"Sure. The sunset is amazing from up here. And there's a new moon tonight, so the stars should be on full display. Make sure you look up from time to time." She smiled and walked through the door, pulling it firmly shut behind her.

As the Forester's engine purred to life and the sound of wheels crunching over rock filled the air, Olivia pocketed the notebook and pencil and turned to Trent.

"We should make a fire while we still have daylight."

He looked at his watch. "I wouldn't mind eating soon. It's been a helluva day."

"*That's* an understatement."

She opened the cooler that sat just inside the door and rifled through it. Leave it to Chelsea. She stood with a grin and two thick packages wrapped in white butcher paper. "How's fresh-caught brook trout sound?"

He rubbed his hands together. "Like heaven. What else is in there?"

She dug through the neatly labeled food stuffs. "Sliced potatoes with onions and peppers." She tossed him the foil packet. "Dried fruit, if you want a snack?"

"Let's save the stuff that doesn't need cooking. Just in case we have to take off."

She nodded her agreement and held up a six-pack of IPA beer. "Thirsty?"

"Tell you what, I'll get the fire going. Why don't you set up the bed and then meet me outside for cocktail hour?"

He swooped down and tucked the six-pack

into the crook of his arm and was out the back door before she could respond. She twitched her lips. She knew what he was doing. He was putting the decision about the sleeping arrangements on her. Clever.

She grabbed the bedding and marched into the back room, expecting to find two twin beds. She did not. She stared at the low-profile queen bed that dominated the tiny square room for a long moment. Her heart pounded a wild rhythm.

Then she shook her head. *Chill.* Sharing a bed didn't *have to* mean anything more. Heck, they'd already spent one night together on her couch and it had been decidedly G-rated. She swallowed around the fluttering in her neck and tossed the blankets and sheets on the bed.

Once the bed was made, she stepped back and eyed it. It looked ... warm. Comfortable. Inviting.

Too inviting?

Like she expected something?

She caught her lower lip between her teeth, then hurried out to the front room and dug through the gear pile, searching for the pair of insulated cocoon-style sleeping bags. She lifted a toiletry pack off the stack and spotted Chelsea's handwriting on an envelope sticking out of the top. She rifled through the pack and removed a package of hand warmers, a package of foot warmers, and the envelope, labeled *'full body warmers.'* She peeked inside and burst out laughing at the sight of an accordion row of condoms. She tucked the envelope into the inner pocket of the windbreaker Chelsea had lent her and resumed her search for the sleeping bags.

She carried the sleeping bags into the bedroom and laid them across the foot of the bed. *Consider it an emergency exit—or a graceful way out,* she told herself. *Just in case.*

She ran a shaking hand through her hair and noted the anticipation dancing in her belly. She remembered the timbre of Trent's voice when he said their kiss meant *everything.* A hot flush crept up her chest to her neck and face. She was pretty sure if anyone was looking for an exit strategy later, it wouldn't be her.

7

Trent poked at the fire with a stick and watched the flame spark and dance. He yawned. The day had been a nonstop adrenaline rush. He was tired. His stomach rumbled. And starving. He pushed the packets of fish and potatoes around on the grate.

The door opened, and Olivia stepped out into the yard. He cracked open a beer and passed it to her as she settled herself next to him on the long log in front of the firepit.

"Cheers." She touched her can to his, then took a long swallow.

He inhaled deeply and scanned the cloudless blue sky. "Looks like your cousin's right about the stars tonight. As clear as it is, with a new moon ..."

"Mmm-hmm."

He frowned. She wasn't looking up at the sky. She was staring off into the middle distance. He was sure she wasn't seeing the trees, though.

"Everything okay?"

"What? Oh, yeah. Just distracted."

"Dinner's about ready. We could eat it out here."

"Yeah, let's do that. I could use the fresh air."

He flipped the fish packets. "Your cousin's pretty clutch in a pinch."

"Yeah, she is. She's the most self-sufficient person I know."

He eyed her. "It must run in the family."

She blinked, surprise sparking in her eyes. "I guess it does. I never really thought of it that way before."

They fell into companionable silence. After a moment she took another sip of beer.

"What about your family?"

His chest tightened. *It's not her fault. She doesn't know.* He flashed back to six-year-old Trent letting himself into an empty apartment with the key he wore around his neck.

"I'm not particularly close with my family. But I guess you could say the way I grew up led me to be pretty self-reliant. We'll leave it at that."

She cringed and hopped to her feet. "I'll get some plates and forks."

"Sounds good." He mustered up a lame smile as she rushed toward the cabin, clearly eager to put some space between them.

She disappeared inside. He drained his beer can and crushed it into a compact circle. Then he cracked his neck—first to the right, then to the left—and took several deep breaths.

When she returned with the dishes, he said, "I'm sorry I snapped. I don't talk about my family."

She held up a hand. "It's okay. I shouldn't have pried."

She turned her attention to pulling the food off the fire, opening the packets, and dumping the contents on to the plates.

"You weren't prying. It's just ... it's a sore subject."

"Okay." She glanced up at him as she handed him a plate. "We're good. But we should eat while the food's still hot."

"Right." He grabbed another beer and dug into the fish.

They ate in silence, and quickly—the way people who've been on the run all day without any food eat. When they'd finished, he took the plates and trash inside. He washed the dishes and forks with quick, efficient movements and placed them in the rack to dry.

He went back outside to find Olivia gazing out at the horizon with her long legs stretched out in front of her. She turned to smile at him. "Thanks for cleaning up. We've probably got twenty minutes or so until the sun sets. You want to sit out here and watch the show?"

"Sounds like a plan to me." He settled next to her and handed her another beer. They sat shoulder to shoulder and looked out at the sky.

"It's hard to imagine someone tried to blow us up today, huh?" Her voice was soft, wondering.

He scowled. Unfortunately, he had no difficulty imaging it.

After a moment, he said, "Tell me about your theory. What do think you're going to learn about Jillian Martin's embassy posts?"

She pulled out the journal and pencil,

balanced the small notebook on her knee, and scribbled a note. "I'm working out a timeline. What date was Carla killed?"

He swallowed hard around the lump that rose in his throat at the memory of Carla's murder.

She looked up at him with sadness in her eyes. "I'm sorry I have to ask this."

He coughed. "No, it's okay. She disappeared the first week of July—the sixth. The box with her hands arrived the next day. Why?"

She answered his question with one of her own. "Do you know when Jillian transferred out of Abuja?"

He shook his head. "She was still there when I left."

"Which was when?"

"Three weeks later. After I found the rest of Carla. I lost control, trashed the place where I was staying. Spent ten days in the brig. Started working for Jake in August."

"And when did Craig Martin join Potomac Private Services?"

He rubbed his palm over his brow and thought. "Sometime in late fall. Mid-November?"

"That tracks. I got the assignment to find out

about Qīng Líng's cell phone tower bids in the northern Mexican states before Thanksgiving. I filed my report in late January. I came back to the States to visit my grandmother in late February, and, well, you know the rest."

"*How* does that track?" He studied her face. What was she seeing that he was missing?

"I keep going back to something Senator Anglin said that night at the lake house. Before you came back from meeting Omar. She was really interested in where you were."

"Okay?"

"You, specifically. She asked for you by name."

He frowned. "Well …. I *am* the only defensive driving instructor at Potomac. And her office called to get you put on the schedule. Jake did it as a favor."

"Right, she called in a favor. Fate didn't put us together in that car that day. Senator Anglin did."

"Hang on, you're saying the entire thing was planned? They *knew* I'd punch out a pilot and drag you off a plane? They *knew* we'd be together when the burn notice came across the wire, and that we'd go on the run? Do you know how farfetched that sounds?"

"I think she would have been fine with the outcome if I'd ended up at the black site at Guantanamo Bay. But once you fought your way onto the plane to save the damsel in distress, she was happy to change courses. I think she secretly expected you to do what you did."

He raised his eyebrows. "It's a stretch."

"Is it? Honestly?"

He bobbed his head from side to side. He *did* have a protective side, and it was widely known at Potomac. The guys called him Sir Mann, the Chivalrous, when they wanted to rile him up.

"Maybe not," he allowed.

"So Craig Martin could have reported to his uncle that you'd try to rescue me."

"Could have. But why?"

She lowered her chin and looked at him fiercely. "I think we both know why."

"You knew too much about QL. And they thought I knew about Senator Townes arranging Carla's murder."

"Exactly."

"So they were trying to kill two birds with one stone," he said dazedly.

They sat in silence for a long moment.

Then she spoke in a voice just above a whisper, "Were? I'd say they still are."

They watched the fiery orange sun dip below the distant mountains as crimson streaks spread out across the purple sky. Once darkness fell completely, which didn't take long in the mountains, he tipped his head back and up to search the sky for constellations, still ruminating on what she said. She leaned forward and poked at the fire.

"I can put on another log."

She shook her head. "No we should go in soon. It's gonna get cold."

"Do you think Ryan is going to be able to find anything solid to pull this all together?"

"I sure hope so. We can't do this for the rest of our lives, can we?"

"I don't know. I think I could."

He nudged her with his shoulder and she leaned in to his chest. He wrapped an arm around her waist and pulled her even closer. They looked up at the stars, pinpoints of light in the immense black night.

When the fire died, she gave a little shiver. "I'm gonna take a quick shower before bed. The smell of smoke in my hair always gives me a headache."

He leaned in and sniffed her head. The smoky aroma mixed with the spicy-sweet scent of Olivia. "It smells pretty good to me."

She punched him lightly on the shoulder and reached across him to grab another beer.

"Shower beer. I approve."

She laughed and headed into the house.

8

Trent sat for a moment longer staring up at the twinkling sky. When he heard the water turn on in the shower, he gathered the empty beer cans and carried them into the house. He tried hard not to imagine Olivia's naked body on the other side of the bathroom door. He failed.

To distract himself from the image, he pawed through the duffel bag full of clothes that Chelsea had grabbed off the racks at her store. He found a pair of dark gray thermal long underwear with a matching long-sleeved shirt in his size and grabbed a similar set in pale blue that looked like it would fit Olivia. He carried them into the bedroom and placed them on the bed.

He spent several minutes looking at the carefully made bed and the sleeping bags laid across the bottom of it, trying to discern the message the tableau was intended to send.

Stop trying to read the tea leaves. Come on, Mann, you're a man of action. Act.

He turned on his heel and walked to the bathroom door, listening to the patter of water. He put his hand against the door and listened to his heart thump faster than the water that pattered against the shower. He inhaled and knocked.

The water turned off, and the door opened. He stepped back. Olivia, still dripping wet, had wrapped an oversized towel around her torso and tucked the end in between her breasts.

"It's all yours."

He watched the hollow in her throat move as she swallowed. Then he lifted his eyes to her face. Her turbulent ocean eyes pierced him with a steady gaze.

He nodded.

"I hope I left you enough hot water."

He smiled.

She smiled back and edged past him, turning

her body toward his as she eased her way through the tight doorway and into the hall.

He stepped inside, closed the door, and rested of his forehead on it. Some man of action. He couldn't even speak, let alone act. It was probably for the best. Sex would only complicate an already messy situation.

He stripped off his clothes, turned the shower on full blast, and stepped into the stream. He lathered up, but no soap could wash away the image of Olivia, naked under that towel, giving him *that* look with those impossibly blue eyes. His body ignored his efforts to tamp down his desire. In desperation, he turned the hot water off and let the icy cold water pound down on him for as long as he could stand it. Then he wrenched off the water, toweled himself off, and wrapped the towel around his waist.

When he stepped into the bedroom, she was sitting cross-legged on the bed, wearing the base layer he'd picked out for her, her damp hair piled in a loose knot on the top of her head.

Somehow, unbelievably, he wanted her even more seeing her in long underwear. He growled, a low rumble in his throat, and cinched his towel more tightly. Then he jutted his chin toward the pajamas.

"Could you toss me those? I'll get dressed in the bathroom and come back for the sleeping bag. You take the bed; I'll bunk out in the kitchen. I don't think there's room on the floor here."

She arched one eyebrow. Her eyes traveled from his face down his bare chest to the towel and back up to his face. She wore a sly half-smile, as if she knew what was going on under his towel. She picked up the long underwear and held them aloft.

"Why don't you come and get them?"

He looked at her for a long moment, then said thickly, "Olivia, you shouldn't start a game if you don't wanna play it."

"Oh, I want to play."

He held her gaze. "Are you sure?"

"I'm sure," she whispered. She wet her lips. "Besides, Chelsea's right, body heat's the best way to stay warm."

She crossed her arms in front her, tugged the hem of her shirt over her head, and tossed it aside. He drank in the sight of her. She smiled and crooked a finger, beckoning him. He dropped the towel to the floor and prowled across the bed. He pushed her gently back onto the bed and eased her pants over her hips. She arched her back and shivered, as he kissed the smooth skin on her belly.

"Looks like we better start generating some body heat," he growled, rising above her.

She reached up and clutched the back of his head, pulling his face down to hers. "I've been waiting for this for a long time. Don't make me wait any longer," she whispered.

He smiled wickedly. "You can't rush genius, Olivia."

Olivia lay curled up in Trent's embrace. His slow, even breathing warmed her neck. His arm was wrapped tightly around her waist and tucked her into his side. He slept soundly, deeply.

He'd earned the rest, she'd give him that. She, on the other hand, was energized. Sated, satisfied, and sore, but wide awake and too wired to sleep. She eased his hand from its spot on her hip and gently, slowly, extricated herself from the bed. She stood silently and crept quietly from the room, stopping to pick up the condom wrappers that littered the floor like confetti. As she padded out to the kitchen, Trent stirred and mumbled.

"Shh, I'll be right back," she soothed.

The floor was cold under her bare feet and she hurried along the hallway. In the dark kitchen, she fumbled with the lantern to light it, then lifted a chair out from the table so as not to scrape it across the floor. She tucked her feet up under her butt and aimed the lantern's glow at the timeline she'd created in Chelsea's notebook.

She was missing something. She narrowed her eyes and studied the list. What was the connection between Qīng Líng and Nigeria? QL sold satellite phones in the West African market, but the company hadn't penetrated the consumer cell phone market in West Africa, or anywhere else on the continent. Yet. She'd seen the ten-year plans in Mateo's office—world dominance was on the menu.

So what did a Chinese cell phone manufacturer/espionage front have to do with a Nigerian jihadist organization? Nothing. She chewed on the end of the pencil for a moment, then she sketched out a series of boxes and labeled them 'QL,' 'Senate Intel,' 'Senate Comm.,' and 'Abuja.' Beneath QL, she wrote 'Mateo, Olivia, Anglin, CNI.' Under Intelligence, she wrote 'Anglin, Townes, CIA.' Under Communications, she wrote 'Anglin, Townes.' And, finally, under Abuja, she wrote 'Townes, Carla, Trent, Jillian, Rear Admiral Sampson.' She drew lines through Carla Ricci's and Lloyd Sampson's names to indicate that they'd been killed. In the margin, she scrawled 'U.S. Marshal Service, Ryan Hayes, Craig Martin, Dane Michaels.'

Then she stared down at the page until her vision blurred and her frustration peaked. She tossed the pencil on the table in disgust. She wasn't going to have an epiphany sitting in a cabin in the Shenandoah Mountains. She needed access to a database, not a flash of inspiration.

A snippet of something Marielle had once told her floated into her consciousness. During their training, Marielle had been assigned a complicated, intricate puzzle to solve. Olivia stopped by Marielle's workstation to see if she wanted to take a break and grab a coffee. She was surprised to see her friend under her desk, stretched out on a soft blanket with a silk sleep mask covering her eyes. When Olivia shook her awake, Marielle cooed, *"Les rêves révèlent tout."*

"Dreams reveal all," Olivia whispered in the cold, quiet kitchen. It had worked for her French friend to untangle a particularly knotty problem; maybe it would work for her. She turned out the lantern, left the book on the table, and tiptoed back into the bedroom.

As she crept back into bed, Trent shifted to make room for her. She reclaimed the spot she'd vacated, snuggling in close to his warm body and resting her head on his chest.

"Everything okay?" He muttered the question with his eyes still closed.

"Better than okay. Sorry I woke you."

He pressed his body more firmly against hers and opened his eyes. "No need to apologize. But if you really want to make it up to me, I have some ideas."

"Oh, yeah?"

"Yeah. You're a little overdressed for what I have in mind though." He smiled slowly.

She popped to her knees and straddled him. Then she stripped off her top in one fluid motion and reached forward to pin his wrists behind his head. She lowered her mouth until it hovered a millimeter above his.

"Better?" she teased.

"Getting there."

He lifted his neck, raising his head far enough to crush his mouth against hers. Her lips parted, and she softened her grip on his wrists. In a flash, he flipped her onto her back and stared down at her with luminous eyes. He trailed a finger along her torso to her waistband.

"Trent," she moaned.

"You hush. I'm on a critical fact-finding mission. This could take a while."

She dropped her head against the pillow, closed her eyes, and melted into his touch.

9
_____

Trent woke to the smell of coffee. As he lay in bed with his eyes still closed, he thought for a bleak moment that he had had yet another dream about Olivia. The most graphic and detailed one yet. But when he opened his eyes and looked blearily around the dark room, the log walls jogged his memory. He bolted upright. Last night hadn't been a dream. It had been very, very real.

He reached around on the floor until he found his pants. He pulled them on and yanked his shirt over his head, then walked out to the bathroom to brush his teeth. His bare feet slapped against the cold wood floor. When he emerged, bright eyed and minty breathed, the cabin's back door hung open, and Olivia stood in the doorway. She held a ceramic mug of coffee in each hand, and the sun framed her from behind with a golden halo.

"Good morning, sunshine," he said.

"Morning." She lowered her eyes, almost shyly.

He crossed the room, took the mug from her left hand and rested it on the floor. Then he cupped her face with his hands and kissed her. "Thanks for the coffee."

She lifted her chin. "Thanks for last night."

Her voice was huskier than usual, and the sound sent a rush of dopamine throughout his body.

"It was, in every sense, my pleasure."

She grinned. "Before you get any ideas, I've got eggs frying over the fire."

"Let me throw on some real clothes. I'll be out in a minute."

"I'll miss you," she teased.

In answer, he brushed his lips over hers and gave her a gentle push out the door. He picked up the coffee and sipped it as he headed to the kitchen to grab the first clothes he found in the duffle bag. As he was lacing his shoes, the door bounced open, and she walked in holding a pan of eggs.

"They cooked faster than expected. Can you grab the coffeepot?" She asked over her shoulder on her way through to the kitchen.

He hurried across the frosty grass to retrieve the pot of coffee from the tree stump that served as a prep table. He filled his lungs with crisp mountain air then headed inside, relieved that no morning-after awkwardness lingered over their gymnastics from the night before. There was a lightness in his chest that he hadn't felt in a long, long time.

They sat at the small table and shared a plate of eggs. Afterward, they moved like dancers around the small kitchen, cleaning up. He brushed up against her whenever he passed her, like a magnet drawn to metal. She poured the last of the coffee into their mugs, and, as he drank, his eyes fell on the little notebook lying upside down on the table.

"May I?" He nodded at the book.

"Please. I looked at it again this morning. I'm missing something."

He scanned the timeline and the flow chart of players that she sketched out. A fragment of a thought poked at him, something important but diffuse. It was just out of reach in the margins of his mind. He grabbed for it, but it slipped through his hands like smoke. He scratched at the stubble that covered his chin after a day without a shave and flipped the page back to the timeline.

"Wait. The timeline starts too late."

Olivia peered over his shoulder. "What do you mean? It starts with the first known event."

"Carla's death."

"Right."

He sipped the coffee. "But she was killed because she learned something, right?"

"Right. My working theory is she found out something about QL and Boko Haram. What, I have no idea."

"Whatever she stumbled into, it happened before July sixth. It must've. Everything that happened afterward all ties back to *that*, not Carla's murder."

Her eyes mirrored the excitement rising in his chest as she grabbed a pencil. "Walk me through it again. Carla got a tip that Boko Haram was going to bomb the embassy, right?"

"Right. There was a local cleric who fed her

information. He's the one who reached out to her."

"How?"

He furrowed his brow. "How?"

"Did he go through an intermediary? A single American woman and a Muslim cleric probably didn't pal around much, did they?"

"Right. They passed messages through an antiquities dealer. Carla used to meet him at the Wuse Market."

"How did she know him?"

He shrugged. "Met him at an embassy dinner. Her cover was that she was an artist. She was always floating around at embassy functions. That's how she met Jillian, too."

"This antiquities dealer, he was Nigerian?"

"No. American, actually. An ex-pat."

"Huh. Were there any Chinese nationals in Carla's circle?"

He closed his eyes and scanned his memory banks, flipping through face after face and name after name. He opened his eyes. "No."

"You're sure?"

"I'm sure. It was my job to know."

"Gotcha." She blew out a breath. "So we need

Ryan to look at Senator Townes' movements and calls in the weeks leading up to July sixth."

He grinned at her. "Right."

"What are you smiling about?"

"We made some forward progress, and Chelsea's not due to come out here for hours. What do you say we balance all this hard work with some play?" He stood and backed her up against the wall.

She arched her head back, and he covered her exposed neck with kisses. She dug her nails into the small of his back and mewed like a kitten. When she caught her breath, she wriggled free and grabbed his hand, tugging him toward the bedroom.

Olivia dreamed of a bustling market. She'd never been to Abuja, so her dream market was Mexico-inspired. In the market, Carla Ricci whispered to a man. Olivia strained to see him, but his face was in the shadows.

She slunk through the market, winding

between the stalls and dodging children running in loud, laughing packs. There!

But, no, he slipped behind a tall, rolled-up rug. Her dream mind itched with frustration. Just turn around. A vendor called to him and he rotated forty-five degrees. Yes, just keep turning. Keep turning—

She started awake, gasping.

Trent looked down at her with concern in his soft hazel eyes. "You okay?"

She got her breathing under control and pushed her hair out of her eyes. "Yeah. Just had a weird dream." She blinked. "What time is it?"

He pulled her toward him, and she rested her cheek on his bare chest. "It's one-thirty in the afternoon. You were out cold."

"Someone wore me out."

"That someone isn't sorry at all." He stroked her hair.

She laughed. "We should get outside, go for a hike, and then have a late lunch. It's Saturday, right?"

"All day long."

"Chelsea has help in the store on weekends. She'll probably come up pretty soon. I can't imagine she'd want to make the drive back down the mountain in the dark."

"A hike, and lunch. Hmm. Okay, we can explore the mountain. But I reserve the right to continue my exploration of Olivia Santos when we get back."

She propped herself up on her elbows. "That can be arranged."

"Good. There are untold treasures yet to be discovered. I can feel it."

She rolled her eyes at his goofiness then froze. *Untold treasures. The man in the dream market.*

She threw off the covers and leapt from bed.

"What's going on?"

"I know who set up Carla. I think I do, at least."

"Who? How?"

She shoved her legs into her jeans and fumbled with the button fly. "There was a guy, another NOC, who was home on leave right before I left for my assignment. My supervisor set up a lunch with him so I could talk to someone who knew the job, lived the life."

"Okay. This was what, three years ago?"

"Yeah, almost four. Anyway, this guy, he'd been in West Africa forever, like a decade. His cover was a treasure hunter. He said the African continent was awash in 'untold treasures.' I remember."

Trent was shaking his head. "I'm confused. A treasure-hunting NOC isn't an antiquities dealer."

She laced up her shoes. "No, he's not. But I heard later, through the grapevine, that he wanted to slow down. Not quit, just do less traveling around. He wanted to be stationary. They stationed him in Nigeria."

"You're sure?"

"I'm positive, but he's not there anymore. When I got approval to come back to the States to see my grandmother, there was some talk about me visiting with the Western Hemisphere desk at Langley. It didn't pan out because the directorate was very busy getting the new MENA director settled in."

"There's a new director of Middle Eastern and North African intelligence? That's a plum position."

"Yeah, it is. And he would've been confirmed by the Senate Intelligence Committee."

"Anglin and Townes."

"Right."

He paced around the bedroom. "You think they rewarded him with the job."

"The timing's too coincidental for it to be anything but quid pro quo. It also explains why I almost ended up in Strawberry Fields, it explains the burn notice, it explains everything. He was manipulating the situation from inside the Agency."

"He's our missing piece."

"The link that ties all the separate threads together."

"We have to get in touch with Ryan."

Before she could answer, the sound of an engine struggling up the mountain filled the air. They raced to the front of the cabin to see Chelsea's SUV lumbering over the rocky terrain. Chelsea lifted a hand in greeting. Olivia made out a silhouette in the back seat and Assistant U.S. Attorney Ryan Hayes sitting next to Chelsea in the passenger seat.

10

"You're just the man we wanted to see," Trent told Ryan before the prosecutor had fully exited the car.

Ryan closed the car door and turned to Trent with a grim expression. "I doubt it."

Trent threw Olivia a puzzled look.

"No, you really are," she chimed in.

Chelsea and the backseat passenger, who turned out to be Leilah Khan, walked over to the cluster looking equally downcast.

A boulder of dread settled in Trent's gut with a thud. "Uh-oh. What's going on?"

"Why don't we make a fire and sit out back and talk?" Chelsea suggested.

"And wait for the others," Leilah added.

"The others?"

She fluttered her long, thick eyelashes innocently. "I told my brother what's going on."

"Leilah—"

"Chelsea didn't say *not* to tell Omar. She just said *to* tell Ryan. So I did both."

Trent sighed. "You said others, plural."

"Omar's bringing Jake and Marielle Moreau," Ryan explained.

"Oh! That's actually good. Elle can help us," Olivia said.

Trent wasn't sure he shared her enthusiasm. Taking down a powerful, shadowy network that was trying to kill you wasn't really a group project. He didn't want to expose these people to danger.

He studied Ryan's face. He knew from Omar's semi-regular card game that Ryan's poker face was strong. Still, he could tell something was wrong.

"Sure, let's have a fire. We have a lot to fill you in on. But, first just tell us what's going on. Something's wrong. Spill it."

Ryan nodded. "I've been removed from the investigation. My replacement is filing a motion to dismiss the indictment against Senator

Townes tomorrow. And I'm off the Anglin case, too."

Trent groaned. "You're kidding."

"I wish. My section chief put me on leave. They want her to fire me."

"Who wants her to fire you?" Olivia probed.

Ryan raised his eyebrows. "Who *doesn't*? The Department of Defense, the Marshals Service, the senators, of course. I'm sure I'm missing a few. I mean, I did harbor a man wanted for the murder of a rear admiral, among my many other missteps. I don't blame them."

Leilah rubbed his shoulder. "It's going to be okay."

He shrugged. "So, you can fill me in, but I'm powerless to do anything. And you're definitely wanted for murder and attempted murder."

"But Leilah told you about Dane Michaels, right? He's dirty," Olivia insisted.

"Dane Michaels is in the wind. Just like Craig Martin. The cases are collapsing, folks."

Trent pressed his palm against his forehead. "I need to think."

Chelsea headed for the back of the cabin. "I'll start the fire."

"I'll help," Leilah offered.

Chelsea laughed. "It's a one-woman job."

"Well, then I'll watch. I've never made a fire before. I want to see how you do it."

Trent nodded. It was completely unsurprising that Leilah, who traipsed to an off-the-grid cabin wearing high-heeled boots, flawlessly applied makeup, and an outfit that probably cost more than Trent's car, was uninitiated in the mysteries of bonfires.

"Come on, we'll all go." Ryan offered Leilah his arm.

Trent and Ryan dragged two more fallen logs over to the circle around the fire cauldron for additional seating while Chelsea stoked the fire and Leilah peppered her with questions. As Trent passed by Olivia, she reached out and laced her fingers through his.

"We'll figure something out," she whispered.

He tucked a tendril of hair behind her ear and brushed his lips over her forehead. "I know."

She was right. They would. But with Ryan sidelined, they'd just lost their best shot at finding out what was going on. Every breakthrough was met with a bigger setback. He settled on the log next to her and draped an arm over her shoulder.

Three sets of eyes registered varying degrees of surprise. Olivia's cousin voiced the unasked question.

"So, you two are, like, a thing now?"

Olivia flushed. Trent cleared his throat. "We are exactly like a thing."

Leilah squealed, and Ryan reached over to clasp him on the shoulder. "Finally."

Chelsea leaned over and stage-whispered, "I hope you found the—"

"—Yes, I found them. *Anyway,*" Olivia said forcefully, "here's what we know."

Trent and Olivia took turns breaking down everything they'd discovered while Ryan peppered them with questions.

Finally, Trent said, "So, in a nutshell, Senator Townes had his niece set Carla up through a CIA intermediary. Carla was murdered, Jillian was transferred to Beijing, and the NOC was promoted. That was stage one."

Olivia picked up the thread, "In stage two, I was misidentified as a Chinese double agent, my cover was burned, and Senator Anglin tried to kill me. When that came to light and I said I'd testify, the bad actors moved into stage three."

"In which the CIA tried to smoke us out by

floating that rumor about Boko Haram. Lloyd Sampson was murdered. When the effort to make it look like suicide failed, I was framed. Olivia found the QL satellite phone with the message from Townes in Carla's things, and you placed her in protective custody."

"One of these bad actors put a hit out on Trent, probably to force your hand, knowing you'd stash him in the safe house with me, giving them the perfect opportunity to take us both out."

"But Olivia's commitment to fitness and healthy living saved our bacon ... and here we are," Trent finished.

From behind, he heard slow clapping. He turned to see Marielle, Jake, and Omar standing in a row beside the cabin.

"That's quite a story," Omar noted, still applauding. "Now, tell us how we can help?"

Beside him, Jake was frozen, staring open-mouthed at Olivia's cousin. Finally, he clamped his mouth shut.

Chelsea paled, and her freckles stood out. "Jake?"

"Chelsea Bishop? *You're* Olivia's cousin?"

～

Olivia pulled Chelsea into the cabin. "What's going on? You look like you've seen a ghost."

"I have," Chelsea mumbled.

"You know Jake West?"

Chelsea rubbed her fingers against her temples as if she were massaging away a tension headache. Then she blew out a breath. "Remember when I took that year off after Berkley and hiked the California Coastal Trail?"

"Yeah. Oregon to Mexico, right?"

"Right. Well, you were doing your CIA training thing at the same time, so you were pretty much unreachable."

She nodded. She recalled getting the odd postcard and maybe a call or two from Chelsea, but otherwise they hadn't been in touch. "Sure."

"I didn't hike it alone. I'd been dating a guy, dating Jake. Nothing serious. It was casual, but we decided to hike the CCT together on a whim."

Olivia winced. "It didn't go well?"

Chelsea closed her eyes. Her voice dropped

low. "No, actually, it went great. It was amazing. We fell in love. Well, I did anyway."

"Chels, what happened?"

She opened her eyes, and tears swam in them. "When we got to Mexico, we splurged on this beachfront resort to celebrate completing the trail. It was amazing. Our last night there, he told me that he'd enlisted in the Air Force and he was leaving for basic training in the morning. We fought. I went down to the bar to drown my sorrows and ended up dancing all night with a pack of sorority sisters from some college in Tennessee. When I dragged myself back to the room as the sun was coming up, Jake was gone."

"He just ... left?"

"Yeah. And I haven't seen him or heard from him since. What's he *doing* here?"

Olivia pressed a finger against her lip and cupped her thumb under her chin while she worked out how to explain. Finally, she said, "Jake's my security consultant. And Trent's boss. He owns Potomac Private Services down on the border with West Virginia."

"I don't understand. He didn't enlist?"

"No, he did. He was a PJ—paramilitary rescue. Air Force Special Warfare, a gray beret.

Trent says he was badly injured during a rescue mission and had to do a ton of rehab. After his discharge, he founded Potomac."

Chelsea shook her head. "I can't believe he's here."

"I can ask him to leave."

"No. It sounds like he has the skill set to help you. I don't. I'll go."

"Chelsea—"

She managed a tremulous smile. "It's okay, really."

Before Olivia could respond, Jake poked his head into the small bedroom. "Can I talk to you for a second?" He locked his eyes on Chelsea.

"Um, sure. I guess."

"I'll give you some privacy." Olivia headed for the door.

"No! Stay!" Chelsea's voice was firm.

"Oh-kay." She pressed herself against the wall and wished she were anywhere else.

"Listen, before you launch into a long story, you should know I'm leaving. We don't need to rehash ... you know." Chelsea lifted her chin and stared defiantly at Jake.

He swallowed audibly. "I disagree. We do

need to rehash ... you know. But this may not be the time. We need your help."

"*My* help?"

"Yeah, your help. Omar has a contact with the U.S. Marshals Service. The DEA partners with them all the time."

Olivia nodded to herself. That made sense.

"Okay?"

"This friend of Omar's says Dane Michaels is a prepper. He has some hidey-hole in Maryland, up near Catoctin Mountain. I'm pretty sure we'll find Craig Martin with him, too. You can help me track them—I know you can."

He wasn't wrong. Chelsea was the perfect partner for the mission. Olivia just wondered if she could bring herself to do it.

As if she sensed Olivia's thoughts, Chelsea fixed her green eyes on Olivia's face and exhaled shakily. "I'll do it for Olivia."

Jake smiled broadly. "Excellent. Thank you. You two should come back outside. We're laying out the plan."

They trailed him through the doorway.

"You don't have to do this," Olivia whispered.

"It's okay, Liv. I want to."

11

Olivia fisted her hands on her hips and breathed fire at Trent. "No way. Absolutely not."

"Olivia—" he began, and that's all the further he got.

"We are not sending our friends into danger while we sit here on a mountaintop and twiddle our thumbs," she raged, her eyes flashing thunder.

He raised both hands. "Let me explain, okay?"

"No."

He caught Marielle's eye and gave her a pleading look. *Handle your best friend, please.*

Marielle sighed. "Stop it, Olivia."

The snap in her voice made Olivia blink. "Pardon?"

"This is a good plan, and you know it is." She jabbed a finger into Olivia's chest. "You're just mad because you'll be stuck here in this cabin. But you are not twiddling your thumbs, you are *not* doing nothing."

Olivia opened her mouth, but Trent jumped in. "Look, you agree that Jake and Chelsea are the right pair to hunt for Martin and Michaels on Catoctin Mountain, right?"

"Yes," she huffed.

"And you agree that the National Archives is on their way, yes? They drive right past DC to get to this mountain?" Marielle persisted.

"Yes."

"So it makes sense for them to drop me and Omar off at the National Archives to use the public computers to run the CREST searches."

"But I could do that," Olivia protested.

"Sure you *could*, but I'll do it better. I see patterns in digital data where nobody else does. It's literally my job, remember?"

"But it's dangerous."

"Which is why she has me," Omar pointed out. "She's the brains, I'm the brawn."

Trent watched as another crack formed in Olivia's armor of resistance and she plopped down on a log.

But she recovered quickly. "So tell me again why we're sending a *prosecutor* to break into a crime scene? That one doesn't make any sense," she insisted.

"I'll field this," Ryan offered. "The Chantilly police aren't plugged in to the federal system. They're unlikely to have heard that I'm *persona non grata* at Main Justice right now. They won't think anything of it if they happen to drive by Lloyd Sampson's place and see me there. His case is still an active homicide investigation, after all. Based on what you and Trent have worked out, Sampson must have had evidence connecting Townes or Anglin to Boko Haram, but he didn't realize its significance. I'll find it. I'll find it fast and get out before anyone knows I'm there."

"And if he doesn't, he has a getaway driver." Leilah beamed at her. "I promise, I can make a quick getaway—even in my brother's giant, stodgy SUV."

Trent crouched near the log where Olivia sat and looked up at her. "Do you think maybe you just don't relish *your* role in all this? Is it that you don't want to talk to Mateo?"

He couldn't blame her. The thought of her calling her ex-husband to weasel information out of him made his gut churn. But she waved away the question.

"No. I mean, sure, I would go to my grave a happy woman if I never, ever spoke to Mateo Flores again. But that's not what's bothering me. We're asking our friends to risk a lot—their jobs, maybe their lives—to help us. I don't want them taking risks that we aren't taking."

"I know." He did. Oh, did he. "You're a leader. Leaders lead. That's what we do. But Olivia, we're wanted for attempted murder. We're fugitives. *We* can't go traipsing into the National Archives or Lloyd Sampson's house. *They* can."

She frowned, and a row of creases lined her forehead. "I don't like it."

"I know, baby, neither do I." He paused. "You know how we talked about being self-reliant last night?"

"Yeah?"

"It's a strength, but it can also be a weakness. This isn't a situation for a lone wolf. It just isn't. There are too many moving pieces. We have friends who want to help us. The strong move here is to let them." He looked around at the six men and women who were willing to put it all on the line for them.

Olivia raised her head and searched their faces, too. At last, she exhaled loudly and stood. "Fine. Somebody leave me a satellite phone, please."

Chelsea hurried forward and slapped a rugged plastic sat phone in Olivia's outstretched palm. "Use mine. Mateo might even recognize the number. I've called your place a time or two over the years."

"Thanks. And Chelsea—all of you—thank you. For all of this." She waved her free hand vaguely, unable to find the words.

"You and Trent would do the same for any one of us," Ryan told her. "And we all know it."

As they watched their closest friends pair up and filter around to the front of the cabin, Trent's chest tightened. He pulled Olivia close and wrapped his arm around her shoulder, drawing as much strength from the connection as he gave to it.

～

O livia eyed the phone like it was a scorpion. For all her bravado with Trent, the thought of calling Mateo turned her stomach and soured her mouth. She swallowed and tasted bile.

Trent studied her face. "You want some water first?"

Yes.

"No."

If she put it off, she'd never do it. She squared her shoulders and punched the number to the villa into the phone. She focused on deep breathing as she listened to the call connect.

"Señor Flores' residence," the dulcet voice of Anita, the house manager, cooed, first in Spanish, then in Mandarin, and, finally, in English.

"Hola, Anita. It's me—Olivia."

Anita, whom Olivia had never once seen at a loss for words, went silent on the other end of the phone.

"Anita? Is Mateo there? I need to speak to him urgently." She cut her eyes toward Trent, who gave her hand an encouraging squeeze.

"Of course, señora. One moment, please."

Señorita, she corrected Anita silently.

As the seconds ticked by, she wondered if Mateo might not take her call. She'd figured his cruel streak would win out over his pride and he'd leap at the chance to berate her. But maybe not? Then what?

Just as she was turning to Trent to tell him the call was a no-go, Mateo's voice boomed in her ear. "Olivia, my apologies for keeping you waiting. I was quite busy with my new bride."

She wanted to gag at the implication but, instead, pasted on a smile and laced her voice with honey. "I hadn't heard you'd remarried. Congratulations, and best wishes to Mrs. Flores."

"Yes, we're very happy. You remember Grace Yáo?"

Her eyebrows hit her hairline. "You married Wang Lei Yáo's daughter?"

Trent shook his head, wondering at the amazement in her voice. She grabbed Chelsea's notebook and wrote: *Daughter of the CEO of Qīng Líng Global. The head honcho.*

Mateo laughed. "Yes, she's quite a step up for me."

The barb barely registered. How had he managed to marry Grace Yáo? The company liked Mateo fine. He got results. But he was an outsider, a foreigner.

"Wow." Her reaction was genuine, so she figured she might as well lean into it.

"Wow, indeed. After ... the incident ... when I had to tell the company that my treacherous wife had been spying on us, I expected my fortunes to dim. Instead, my star rose."

"It did?" She wrinkled her brow. That made no sense.

"They valued my honesty. And they understood that I was not to blame for your duplicity. In fact, I'm being promoted."

"You are?" She realized she sounded like an airhead, but that didn't seem to bother her ex-husband.

"I am. Next month, Grace and I leave for my new post in Lagos."

"Lagos?" she parroted.

"It's in Nigeria," he said as if speaking to a small child.

"I know where it is, Mateo," she snapped. "But I thought QL didn't have any immediate plans for a West African presence."

"Ah, yes, not in the consumer market. That's true. But I'm heading up a new, very important project. Top-secret." His oily voice took on an extra layer of self-satisfied smarm.

She stifled a sigh and played along. "Oooh, that sounds fascinating. I'll bet it's something really special. Like two-way radios."

She smiled to herself for getting in the dig. Mateo had famously championed two-way radios in the Mexican market, and the idea had bombed. It was his greatest failure.

"No, you dolt. Not two-way radios. Military communications for the Nigerian military." He virtually screamed at her, and then the line went silent as he realized he'd said too much.

She waited a beat, then said, "Eh, that doesn't sound very exciting to me."

He jumped on the bait. "Yes, of course. It really isn't. It's not even truly a promotion. More of a lateral move. But Grace, she wants to live in Lagos, she loves the city. And as you Americans say, happy wife, happy life."

"Happy wife, happy life," she echoed.

"Why did you call, anyway?" His tone sharpened. He was ready to be done. That was fine with her. She'd gotten more than she'd ever dreamed she would.

"My grandmother's hope chest. You know,

the domed trunk in the attic? Could you please send it to my lawyer? I'll reimburse you for the cost of shipping, of course."

"I'll leave instructions for Anita to forward all your remaining belongings before she lists the villa for sale."

"Thank you."

"Of course. But, Olivia?"

"Yes?"

"I wouldn't hold out hope of using that hope chest. I can't imagine any man would want you now. So brittle and dried up."

Having gotten the last word, Mateo slammed the phone down in her ear.

12

"Did you catch all that?"

Trent nodded. He had. That prick.

"You know he's wrong—about whether you're desirable or not. Because I assure—"

"Mateo's words lost the power to affect me years ago. Forget about that. Did you hear what he said about Nigeria?"

He eyed her carefully. It seemed impossible that Olivia could be so nonchalant about her ex-husband's meanness, but apparently she was. She looked back at him wide-eyed, waiting for an answer.

"Yeah, I heard it. I know, there are no coincidences, but all it does is introduce yet another loose end that we have to wrap up."

She shook her head. "I don't think so. I think it's the key."

"His new job is the key?"

"Yeah, but we need to get out of here. Fast. Grab a flashlight and the first aid kit. Oh, and the waterproof matches. Just grab whatever you can." She raced around the kitchen, throwing food and layers of clothing into one of the backpacks.

"Whoa, whoa, slow down."

She wheeled around, shaking her head. "No, we can't slow down. Hurry up, please. Langley's only sixty or seventy miles away at best. They could have a chopper here in twenty minutes."

"Why would the CIA send a helicopter here, Olivia?" He caught her by the arm. "Take a breath and tell me what you're thinking."

She inhaled deeply and then exhaled a long, slow breath. When she spoke her speech was less frenetic, more measured.

"There. I took a breath. Happy now? Please get some stuff together. I'll explain while we pack."

"Okay," he agreed, grabbing the backpack she tossed him.

"I'm positive the Chinese government was monitoring my call with Mateo."

He shoved a handful of energy bars into the bag. "That's plausible."

"Grace Yáo's family is wildly powerful. And the CIA is almost certain her father's a Chinese spy. So let's go with definite rather than plausible." She pulled on a waterproof jacket while she explained.

"Okay, Beijing heard your call."

"And likely can pinpoint where we are. They know where we are, Trent."

He believed she was right. But he was still missing something. "And that information gets to Langley how, exactly?"

"The guy running the MENA Division. He's not working for Boko Haram or even Senator Townes—he's a Chinese agent. He's gotta be. It's all connected, and we have to go. Now."

She tossed Chelsea's sat phone on the table and took one final look around. "I hate to run without a phone but we can't risk bringing that."

Trent smiled. "I have a surprise for you."

She blinked. "What kind of surprise?"

"The burner phone kind." He reached into his pocket and pulled out the cheap flip phone Omar had given him.

"When? How?"

"While you and Chelsea were in here having your heart-to-heart, Omar passed them out. He had four. He has one, I have one, Ryan has one, and Jake has the last one."

"Who walks around with four virgin burners?"

"He's undercover with the DEA, Olivia. He probably buys them in bulk."

"Fair enough. You can call them once we're a safe distance from the house."

They ran through the house and out the back door. When they reached the edge of the clearing, Olivia stopped. "The falls are to the east. There should be an access road for the rangers on the other side. We'll have to go through the river, though. That's good to dilute our scent if they bring dogs, but bad because we'll be cold and wet."

"What's to the west?"

"I have no idea."

"I don't think getting soaked is a smart move—not if there's a chance we'll be sleeping in the woods tonight." He'd been a Navy SEAL. Being wet and cold had at one time been his *raison d'être*, but there was no reason to subject Olivia to those conditions if they could be avoided.

"West it is," she agreed.

They followed the Ridgeline for about two miles until they reached a craggy ravine. He lay on his stomach and peered over the edge. "It's steep and rocky, but the stream looks shallow. If we're crossing, we should do it here."

She joined him, hanging over the cliff, and scanned the crevice. "Okay, let's do it. But let's make those calls first. *If* we're going to have reception, which is a long shot, it'll be better up here than down in the gorge."

He pulled out the phone and powered it on. They bent their heads over the small screen and watched the thing boot up, search for a signal, and fail. He met her eyes and vowed, "We'll find a way to contact them."

She nodded, but he could see the doubt in her eyes. He stowed the phone, then reached out and traced the curve of her cheek with his thumb. "I promise."

She caught his hand with hers. "Don't do

that. You can't guarantee that. I want to know when you promise me something, it's real."

He kissed her hard. "I am promising you something real. We *will* get in touch with the others. And you can know that every vow I make will hold. Understand?"

Her eyes watered, and he thought she might cry, but she blinked hard, twice, and smiled. "I understand."

The distant *thwack, thwack, thwack* of a heli-copter's blades sounded. Trent and Olivia jumped to their feet and scanned the horizon.

"If we hijack it, could you fly it?" she asked hopefully.

Leaving aside the prospect of a shootout with an indeterminate number of CIA agents, commandeering the chopper would be problem-atic at best.

"*Could* I try? Maybe. *Should* I? No. I was a SEAL, remember? Navy, not Air Force. Jake could, for sure."

She twisted her lips into an uncertain bow. "Yeah. Too bad. Let's hit it."

"You go first. Go slow."

She lowered herself into the crevice and found her footing. She downclimbed sideways, searching for her next hold as she inched down the steep rockface. He watched her progress until she'd descended about seven feet. The helicopter's blades grew louder.

He gripped the lip of the ravine and dropped down to the first ledge. "You good down there?" He called.

She looked up from below. "I'm good. Just don't fall on me."

They worked their way down, one foot at a time. By the time he dropped to his feet beside her, his shirt was slick with sweat. She shook out her hands.

"Ah, that was no fun. I have a cramp in my left hand."

"Here."

He encircled her left hand with his and massaged her wrist and the pressure points in her palm.

"Thanks."

"Want me to do the other one?"

She parted her lips to answer, and a twig cracked to the right, just around a bend in the wall. Olivia swung around, already pulling her gun from the holster.

His was in his hand in an instant, safety off,

aiming at the blind corner. His heart was a steady thrum. His hand was rock solid. He breathed in, then out. Ready.

A woman stepped into view and gestured with a handgun of her own. "Put those damn fool things away," she ordered.

"Nicole?" Olivia gaped.

Trent squinted into the afternoon sun. Yep, Deputy Marshal Nicole Reese stood on the stream bank, pointing her government-issued weapon at Olivia's center mass.

13

The sun glinted off Nicole's gun, strangely beautiful. Up on the ridge, the sound of a helicopter touching down filled the air. To Olivia's left, the stream burbled past. The cool air brushed over Olivia's skin, feather soft. And the faintly sweet scent of silt loam filled her nose.

She focused on each of these sensory details for a moment to ground her in the here and now, to slow her response, to lower her pulse rate. After a long moment, she spoke in a calm, clear voice.

"I'm going to tuck my gun back in my hip holster, okay, Nicole? The safety is on."

She kept her eyes on the deputy marshal's

face while she slowly holstered her weapon. Then she held up her hands. "See?"

"Good girl. Your turn." Nicole jerked her head toward Trent.

Olivia turned and saw him press his lips together and pull back his head. Reluctant, unwilling, challenging.

"Trent, do it."

"Please listen to her, Mr. Mann. I'll put mine away as soon as you do. You have my word."

Trent searched her face and must have found something to reassure him because he nodded, engaged the safety, and stowed his weapon.

"Good."

As promised, the deputy marshal returned her gun to her shoulder holster, and Olivia exhaled. Trent stepped forward and stood next to her, his left shoulder touching her right.

"Nicole, we had nothing to do with that explosion. You must know that," Olivia tried to reason with the woman.

"I know you ran."

"Your partner tried to kill us!"

Tsk. Nicole clicked her tongue. "You think I didn't figure that one out? But you two made me look stupid, not Michaels."

"He was willing to kill you, too," Olivia pointed out.

"I *know*."

"If you know, then why does the Marshal Service have our faces plastered all over creation? Why are we wanted for your attempted murder? Especially since your partner cut and run. Doesn't that seem suspicious to anybody else in your agency?" Trent wanted to know.

"Ah, now those are good questions. The answer is this rot runs deep. Somebody high up is calling the shots."

Olivia nudged Trent.

Nicole noticed and nodded. "But you already know that."

"Yeah."

"How did you find us?" Trent asked.

"I'm a United States Marshal. Didn't you ever watch 'The Fugitive?'" She snorted.

"Seriously, Nicole."

"Seriously, I'll tell you all about it while we hike our asses out of this ravine. I assume you don't want to be pinned down here when whoever's in that helicopter comes looking for you."

She had a point. "Lead the way."

Nicole held up her hand like a crossing

guard. "Now, before I turn my back on the two of you, I want to make sure we're straight. I pulled my gun on you because I know who you two are and what you're capable of—especially when cornered. But I'm a friend. I'm here to help."

"So you're saying you come in peace," Olivia cracked.

"I do," she responded seriously.

Olivia met her eyes. "We lived together for over a month. I know who you are."

Nicole smiled. "Thanks for that. 'Course I thought I knew who Dane was, and look how that turned out."

"Hey," Trent said, "you're not Dane. You're good people, deputy."

"Flatterer."

Nicole led them to the bend in the stream, where they crossed over and mounted a rocky embankment dotted with lush green trees. The sound of rushing water grew louder as they hiked.

"Will we pass the falls?" Olivia asked.

"No. Have to wade through the river if you go that way. That's a fool's game."

Trent chuckled.

"So tell us how you found us," Olivia prompted.

"Girl, whatever evil mastermind is out to get you two did do one thing right. That reward has the phone lines jumping. Most of them are cranks, but I got this call from a guy running an unlicensed cab out of the bus station at the Rosslyn Metro—"

"Arjun? I'm hurt. We paid him a hundred bucks. I talked baseball and recipes with him!" Olivia was only half-joking.

"If it's any consolation, he liked you a lot. But money's money. He told me where he dropped you off. And I took my little self to Bordman's Biscuits and Breads and surveyed that parking lot. Seemed curious to get dropped off at the edge of town like that. For a minute, I thought you might have hightailed it up to your family's lake house. Then I spotted that rail trail running behind the factory and I knew where you'd gone. You asked your cousin for help."

Olivia frowned and searched her memory. "How did you know about Chelsea? We never talked about her, did we?"

"No, but on the initial report, Ryan listed your closest contacts. Chelsea Bishop was one of them. So, I used my big old brain and connected the dots. By the time I got to her store this afternoon, she'd already left." She paused and shook her head in disbelief. "This next part was good old-fashioned luck. I'm cruising through town, real slow, just to get a feel for the place, and who do I see getting into an SUV out in front of some Irish pub? None other than AUSA Hayes and a drop-dead gorgeous Middle Eastern woman. I didn't know it was your cousin's car at that point. But I got curious about Hayes and followed them."

"You're kidding," Olivia blurted.

"Luck's a big part of this job. Sometimes it breaks for you, sometimes it breaks against you. Today was my day."

"If you followed everyone to the cabin, why didn't you apprehend us there?" Trent asked.

"Let's see, for one thing, there were six of you and one of me."

"You could've called for backup."

She stopped climbing and spun to face him. "Are you for real? You honestly think I'm here to capture you and bring you in? No. First, my partner tried to kill you—kill us, actually. Second, now you're being set up by my agency.

That doesn't sit right with me. I'm gonna *help* you. So I didn't come busting into the cabin because I don't want a soul back in D.C. to know I found you."

"You'll really help us?"

"Of course I will. I have an all-terrain vehicle parked in a clearing about three miles from here."

Olivia eyed her. "And?"

"And we're gonna drive it to the trailhead where I left my car. I'll drop you off, and you can borrow my car. We'll worry about the details of getting it back to me later."

"Nicole, thank you!" Olivia threw her arms around the deputy marshal and hugged her tight.

Nicole stiffened and patted her woodenly on her back. "Now don't go getting mushy on me."

"Hang on. Have you thought this through?" Trent interjected. "Don't get me wrong, we need the help. But you're probably destroying your career right now, Deputy Marshal Reese. Lending us a vehicle could open you up to additional criminal charges."

She waved a hand. "Ryan Hayes is helping you, right? If he's not worried, I'm not worried.

Besides, I'm done with the marshals. I never thought I'd say that, but those SOBs are gonna let Dane get away with trying to kill me? Uh-uh. No thank you. I've already called an employment lawyer to help me handle my exit. The Marshals Service will be settling with me so fast that check'll leave skid marks in their bank account."

"If you're sure about that, you should think about coming to work for Potomac. Jake is always looking for smart, tenacious people with ethics. It's a smaller population than you might think."

Nicole grinned. "No thanks. I'm done with the security industry. I'm going to follow my bliss in my next chapter."

"Which is?"

"Nicole's Bliss, a vegan cupcakery."

"Really?"

"Wait until you taste my strawberry cupcakes. You'll see. Now get your rears in gear. I want to get out of these woods before the sun sets."

She doubled her pace, and they followed suit.

14

Nicole's strawberry cupcakes did not disappoint. Trent and Olivia sat in Nicole's spotless sedan and polished off the care package she'd handed them before zooming off on the ATV.

"Hard to believe these are vegan," Olivia murmured, licking her fingers.

"Hard to believe Nicole Reese just gave us her car," he countered.

Olivia dabbed frosting from the corner of her mouth and cocked her head. "I don't know. I think Dane's willingness to kill her was a clarifying moment. I'm just glad she's getting out now. The world deserves these cupcakes."

Trent grinned at her lighthearted mood. She

was right to feel optimistic. They had food, wheels, and a cell phone signal. And, most importantly, the inkling of an actual plan.

"Now that you've finished your dessert, we should make some calls."

He flipped open the phone, activated the speaker, and jabbed speed dial 1. She leaned over and peered at the display.

"Who are you calling first?"

"Beats me," he shrugged. "Omar programmed in the numbers but didn't label them. It's better this way. Less evidence. Besides, it doesn't matter. We need to talk to everyone."

The phone rang twice, then Ryan picked up, speaking in a loud whisper. "Hayes."

"It's Mann. Why are you whispering?"

"I don't know. I'm not an experienced cat burglar."

"I'm here, too. You're on speaker," Olivia interjected. "How's it going?"

"We're at Sampson's house. Leilah's got the Suburban idling in that turnaround out front. I've searched his library, his closet, and his bedroom and have come up empty. I was just about to admit defeat and get out of here, unless you have any brilliant ideas."

Trent closed his eyes and pictured Lloyd Sampson. The last time he'd seen the man, Sampson had been shuffling around his mansion in leather slippers, sucking down expensive bourbon. He opened his eyes.

"In the library, you went through his desk drawers and bookshelves, right?"

"Sure."

"Did you check the bar cart?"

"What?"

"There's a silver bar cart by the windows. See if there's anything in the drawers."

"Hang on."

Ryan placed the phone down, and Trent listened to him banging around.

A moment later, Ryan was back, breathless and excited. "Hot damn. The drawers were a bust, but I laid down on the carpet and felt around on the underside of the cart. Sure enough, there was a manila envelope taped to the bottom."

Trent pumped his fist. Beside him, Olivia bounced in her seat.

"Open it."

"Simmer down, I am." The sound of rustling

paper came across the line, then, "Okay, it's some kind of security training and education initiative between the U.S. military and the Nigerian military. There's a joint special forces group that's supposed to advise and assist the Nigerians with expanding their own special forces. I'm skimming —a lot of these acronyms are meaningless to me."

"It's okay, keep going."

"There's a program specific to fighting Boko Haram."

Olivia snapped her fingers. "Back when the rumor about the U.S. partnering with Boko Haram was floating around, I read an article in the Australian press about a similar training program between the Aussies and the military in Niger. The spokesperson was criticizing the idea of the U.S. backing Boko Haram, which, clearly was ludicrous. But I think I know how the rumor might have started."

"Well, don't hold out on us," Trent said.

"Ryan, does the directive include any provisions for selling the Nigerians equipment? That's fairly standard in these training and education programs, right?"

"Right," Trent confirmed, "We partner with

the foreign government, sell their military the equipment, then train them on how to use it."

The sound of flipping pages crackled the tinny speaker. "Uh, no ... I don't see a sales component here."

"That's odd," Trent mused. The equipment sales were a big money-maker.

"I know why," Olivia explained. "The Nigerian government is buying the equipment from QL. Probably at a huge discount. That's why Mateo's being transferred to Lagos. QL is, no doubt, offering the equipment so cheaply because they have a side deal with Boko Haram to spy on the military and report their movements."

Ryan swore softly.

"That's depraved," Trent said. He balled his fists and pushed down his rising anger. The lives of all those Nigerian soldiers were at risk.

"It is. And, if we're lucky, Marielle and Omar are going to find a paper trail that shows the CIA and the Senate Intelligence Committee knew about it."

"So Sampson was killed because they were afraid he'd connect the dots between Carla's murder and this program," Trent mused.

"Right. The common denominator is—"

"Townes," they said in unison.

Trent's chest ached. "And Carla figured it out. Or came close. So Townes had her executed."

Olivia reached across the center console and squeezed his hand. He lifted her hand to his mouth and kissed it.

"Ry—" The sound of crashing glass drowned out whatever Olivia had been about to say.

"Hayes, you okay?"

"Somebody's here."

"The police?"

"Don't think so. They wouldn't have smashed the kitchen door to get in."

"Go. Now. Take that envelope and get the hell out of there."

"Roger that."

He ended the call. Trent stared at Olivia, his heart racing.

"He'll be okay. Remember, Leilah's his wheelman."

"Wheelwoman, you mean."

"Fair point. But they're going to be okay," she assured him.

He smiled tightly. He'd sent Ryan and Leilah to the house because they were a pair of civilians and it seemed like the safest mission. If his judgment was wrong, whatever happened to them would be on him.

Olivia eyed him with concern.

"You're right."

"I am. And, look we're still a step ahead of the bad guys."

"Barely," he countered, grimly.

"We don't have to win by a mile. Counterespionage is a game of inches. Come on, start driving. I'll call the others from the road."

He nodded and turned the key in the ignition. They were running out of time.

Olivia hit the number 2 on the speed dial while Trent careened around a corner. She gripped the handle set in the car's ceiling with her right hand and held the phone in her left.

"West." Jake's voice crackled.

"It's Trent and Olivia. Where are you two?"

"We dropped Omar and Marielle at the National Archives thirty or so minutes ago. Apparently, the residents of the District of

Columbia didn't get the memo that today is a Saturday. We're sitting in snarled traffic on the George Washington Parkway. We're probably still an hour away from Catoctin Mountain." His frustration oozed through the handset.

"Chelsea, how are you doing?" Olivia asked.

"Fine. I'm studying this map of Catoctin Mountain, though, and I'm not sure how we're going to find Michaels' camp before nightfall." She was all business.

"That's why we're calling. We got a lead. See Cunningham Falls State Park on your map—just to the south of Catoctin Mountain Park, the part owned by the National Park Service?"

"Yeah."

"The two parks are adjacent, but there's a slice of land in the southeast corner where the boundary gets wavy."

"I see it."

"That piece of land is privately owned. Michaels has his camp there."

"That's a pretty specific lead," Jake observed. "Mind sharing your source?"

Olivia and Trent exchanged a look. Then Trent said, "Michaels' partner. A deputy marshal."

"You sure we're not walking into a trap?"

"No, I'm not *sure*. But we trust her. She lent us her car. We're on our way to provide backup."

"Bad idea, buddy. You're a wanted man, remember?"

"The plan was for you two to stay put at the cabin," Chelsea protested.

"The plan changed. The CIA got a bead on our location and sent out a chopper. We had to run."

"How is that possible?"

"Their inside guy isn't working with Boko Haram, at least, not directly. He's working with the Chinese."

"The Chinese government?"

"Qīng Líng, but, you know ..."

"There's not much daylight between Beijing and QL."

"Exactly."

"Well, crap. Don't bring the CIA with you."

"We'll try not to," she promised.

"Wait, if the Marshals and the CIA can't be trusted, what are we supposed to do if we find these guys and their camp? Make a citizen's arrest?" Chelsea asked.

Trent leaned forward. "I have a plan."

"Care to share it?"

"When we see you. Let's meet at the Cunningham Falls Visitors Center."

He shot Olivia a look and drew his finger across his neck.

"Bye, you two. Be careful."

She ended the call and eyed Trent. "Care to share this plan with me?"

His cheek twitched. "I'd rather not just yet. It's still a work in progress. Besides, you have one more call to make."

That response wasn't particularly comforting. She narrowed her eyes and gave him a suspicious look. He whistled and focused on the road. She muttered under her breath but punched speed dial 3.

"Allo?" Marielle trilled.

"Hi, it's me. How's it going?"

"We're all finished here."

Trent's eyebrows shot up his forehead. "Already?"

Omar chimed in, "She's magical, man. You should've seen her tease out the information she wanted. Needles, haystacks, they have nothing on Elle."

Elle? Hmm. As far as Olivia knew, she was the only person permitted to call Marielle 'Elle.'

"So, what are you doing now?"

"Omar is insisting that I eat food prepared in and sold from a truck. This mission is more dangerous than I even imagined," Marielle joked.

"Best empanadas in the District," Omar insisted.

"What is this—a field trip?" Trent griped.

"Dude, relax. We don't have a car, remember? Jake dropped us off. I'm not sure *how* off radar we need to stay, so we were gonna grab a bite and then call you. Do we call for a ride share? Take the Orange Line to Northern Virginia and then call somebody for a lift? Rent a car?"

"No, take the Red Line to Friendship Heights. My Aunt Hailey's got a place just off Wisconsin Avenue in Chevy Chase. She's out of town, but you can use her station wagon. I'll text you the address and the code to get into the garage. The keys are hanging on a pegboard by the light switch," Olivia instructed.

"Great. Where are we going? Back to the cabin?"

"No. The cabin's been compromised, which also means you need to stay *way* off the radar."

"Got it. So where do we rendezvous?"

Trent clicked his tongue, thinking. "Call your sister. She and Ryan had to run from Sampson's house. Make sure they don't need help, and then the four of you figure out a safe meeting place."

"What do you mean, they had to run?" Omar went into big brother mode.

"Ryan was inside the house and someone busted out the glass in the kitchen door. He went out the front, Leilah already had the car running. I'm sure they're fine, but just check in with them, okay?"

Trent spoke in a measured voice, but Olivia could tell he was berating himself for exposing Ryan and Leilah to danger.

"Where are you two?" Omar asked in a calmer tone.

"We're headed to Maryland to back up Jake and Chelsea."

Marielle interrupted, "Does *nobody* want to hear what I found?"

Olivia could hear the pout through the phone. "I absolutely want to hear."

"Finally! The CREST searches were useless. All the good stuff was blacked out of the reports."

"Told ya," Trent snarked.

Olivia shook her head. "So what did you find?"

"Embassy press releases for various social events. Some people were very sloppy about allowing themselves to be photographed."

The note of triumph ringing in Marielle's voice sent an excited shiver along Olivia's spine. "What've you got?"

"Jillian Martin at a black-tie gala in Abuja, she's standing next to Carla Ricci. But off to the right, still in the frame, is Ron Cumberland. It's clear that the three of them were talking together just before the photographer snapped the shot."

"Who's Cumberland?" Trent asked.

"The former NOC who was in West Africa for ages and is now the section chief for MENA."

"That's solid," Olivia told her.

"But, wait, there's more," Omar promised.

"I like how your friend has her own hype man," Trent said as an aside to Olivia.

"I know, right?"

"There are more photographs from a New Year's party at the U.S. embassy in Beijing."

"Like a Lunar New Year party in February? That's too late to work for our timing."

"No, Liv, the last day of December. And who do you think posed with their champagne flutes and glittery party hats? Jillian Martin, again. Again with Cumberland. But this time, she's also with her uncle, the senator, and Grace Yáo and her dad."

Olivia's throat went dry. Adrenaline zinged through her bloodstream. She swallowed hard and exhaled slowly. "Marielle, that's great. Amazing. You have to be very, *very* careful, okay? Cumberland has a direct line to the Yáos. And, by the way, Mateo and Grace Yáo are apparently married now. Within a half an hour of my hanging up with Mateo, there was a chopper outside the cabin."

Omar whistled. "We gotta get off the street."

"Yeah, maybe take a rain check on those empanadas," Olivia suggested

Trent frowned at the phone. "Stay frosty, Khan."

15

Trent pushed Nicole Reese's car to its limits, Olivia gripped the grab handle like it was her job, and they pulled into the parking lot at Cunningham Falls one hour and four minutes after they'd finished their cupcakes. It wasn't a personal best, but he was satisfied that he'd expertly threaded the needle between speed and not being pulled over by a state trooper.

"Whew, that road was twisty," Olivia groused.

Trent wore the complaint as a badge of honor. He scanned the lot for Chelsea's Forester as he killed the engine. "Looks like we beat Jake and Chelsea here."

"We didn't have D.C. traffic to contend with."

"That's true."

"We could pass the time with you telling me about your plan in progress," she suggested.

"Eh. We could. Or ..."

"Or?"

He grinned at her. "You told me to pack up whatever I could find back at the cabin."

"Yeah, I remember. So?"

"I wasn't sure if we'd be spending the night outdoors, so I grabbed the full body warmers." He raised an eyebrow.

She stared at him for a few seconds then burst into laughter. "You found that envelope?"

"Your cousin must've been a Girl Scout, always prepared."

Her laughter faded. "I don't think she was prepared to see Jake walk back into her life."

He eyed her, the mostly joking offer of a quickie forgotten. "Yeah. I didn't get the whole story, but it sounds like she really broke his heart."

"*She* broke *his* heart?"

Uh-oh.

"I'm guessing you heard it differently."

"Mmm-hmm."

The temperature in the car plummeted about

ten degrees. If she got any frostier, he really would need a body warmer, but not the kind he had in mind. He cast about for a safer topic and, finally, in desperation blurted his plan.

"Chelsea's right that we need a way to bring in Martin and Michaels and we can't just call the local authorities and hope for the best."

"We could kill them."

He froze and gave her a sidelong look.

"Relax, I'm kidding!"

"Whew, okay. I was worried."

"Yeah, I could tell. So, what's your non-murderous plan?"

"It involves lying," he said to test the waters.

"Trent, I operated under non-official cover for three years. Lying is like breathing."

"Are you sure that's the message you want to deliver to a guy at the outset of a new relationship?"

"When the guy was one-half of an undercover team on the Black Squadron, yeah, I'm comfortable with that message."

He laughed darkly. "Okay, that's fair. But let's make a deal. We may both be professional liars, but this ... us ... is different, right?"

Her expression softened, and she leaned in

close to him. "Trent Mann, I will always be honest with you about us."

He was once again in danger of drowning in her eyes. "Good," he whispered. "So will I. Always."

They moved toward one another, meeting in the middle, and sealed their agreement with a long, hard kiss. Her lips parted to accept his tongue, and he raked his hands through her glossy hair.

A sharp knock sounded on the driver's side window, and they both jumped, knocking their foreheads together.

"Get a room," Chelsea shouted from the parking lot while Jake pointed and laughed.

"Those two deserve each other," Trent grumbled, rubbing his head as he exited the car.

The four of them clustered together in the parking lot between the two vehicles.

Trent took charge. "Here's the plan. After we pinpoint Dane Michaels' and Craig Martin's location, we wander over to the border of Camp David."

"What?" Chelsea asked.

"The presidential retreat is somewhere within Catoctin Mountain Park. It's not on any of the maps, but it's visible on satellite," Olivia explained.

"And it's pretty easy to figure out exactly where it is. If you hike too close to it, very polite Marines holding automatic weapons will ask you to leave," Trent added.

"When the president's there?"

"No, all the time," Trent assured her. "So we draw the attention of the Marines and tell them two men in a cabin near Cunningham Falls have been bragging about how they've managed to break into Camp David repeatedly."

"And, what, the Marines are going to storm Michaels' cabin?" Jake asked.

"Yes."

"What if they don't?"

"They will."

"And then what?"

"Once we get them there, we simply explain the truth. Martin and Michaels are implicated in multiple murders and they're spying for the Chinese. They'll take it from there."

"That's absurd," Jake declared.

"Absurd, really?"

"Okay, do you like ludicrous better? Preposterous? Ridiculous?"

Trent clenched his jaw.

"Hang on," Olivia said, positioning herself between the two men. "Tensions are running a bit high. Let's just calm down."

"Why do you think this Marine Security Force is going to do your bidding, Trent?" Jake wanted to know.

"Well, because they're patriots. But also because Camp David is officially a naval installation. Those Marines report to a commander in the United States Navy. Once he hears that they're responsible for the murder of Rear Admiral Sampson, trust me, Martin and Michaels will be dealt with."

Chelsea sat on a low stone wall, swinging her legs. "I'll be honest, it sounds like a decent plan to me."

Jake threw up his hands. "I guess it's marginally better than *no* plan."

"You're just feeling left out because the fly boys can't come to our rescue," Trent jabbed him.

"Sure, that's it. This is just an old military branch rivalry," Jake snarked.

Olivia clapped her hands together. "Now that that's settled, why don't we enact the first step of this plan and find the freaking cabin?"

Finding the cabin was laughably easy for Jake and Chelsea. Olivia and Trent hung back a few steps and let the other two jabber about flattened grass, broken plants, and shoe prints. Chelsea saw something that made her run ahead to the rise. She stood on a flat rock and scanned the valley below through her field binoculars.

After a moment, she turned and waved her arms. Trent, Olivia, and Jake jogged up to the rock.

"Whatcha' got?" Jake asked, taking out his own binoculars.

"Behind that copse of beech trees, there's a structure."

Trent squinted through the screen of tall, skinny trees and their early spring leaves. He was about to shake his head and say he didn't see it, when a flash of light glinted off a square of glass. "I see it. There's a window."

"Fools used glass," Jake shook his head, then turned to Chelsea with a wide grin. "Nice work."

Chelsea flushed bright red. "Thanks."

"Wow, and I thought you were a blusher," Trent said to Olivia.

She tented her eyebrows and twisted her lips into a smirk. "Who, me?"

"Yes, you. I can demonstrate."

He reached into his jacket pocket, mouthing 'condoms.' She batted his hand away as the tell-tale pink stains traveled up her neck to her cheeks.

"I rest my case."

Jake turned to them. "Stop screwing around back there. We need to figure out our approach, and we need to do it quietly."

He was right. The cabin seemed distant, separated by the steep mountain and the row of trees. But in truth, it was closer than it looked.

Trent cleared his throat and whispered. "Olivia and Chelsea should go draw the patrol's attention near Camp David now."

"Olivia and Chelsea?" Olivia echoed softly. "How about Trent and Jake? *You two* are their brothers in arms or whatever, not us."

"Yeah, but you two are cuter. And less likely to be shot on sight," Jake countered, as Chelsea blushed uselessly.

Olivia jutted out her chin. "This plan sucks. I

didn't come all this way to run an errand while you two take down Michaels and Martin," she snapped.

Trent sighed heavily. He'd known this was going to be a sticking point. But he didn't see a clear compromise that they could all live with. "Look—"

A spray of bullets peppered the trees behind them and the crack of a gunfire sounded in the valley.

"Take cover!"

Jake knocked Chelsea to the ground and covered her body with his. Olivia hit the ground and elbow-crawled to the front of the rock. She propped herself on her elbows and aimed her 45 into the valley.

Trent stepped to his right, taking cover behind an aspen tree, and readied his 9mm. The handgun wasn't his distance weapon of choice, but assuming the shooter or shooters were taking cover near the cabin, he only had to cover eighty meters or so. And he had the high ground. And the knowledge that he was a better shot than just about anybody on the planet—or at least in North America. He liked his odds.

Another volley of bullets sprayed the trees,

giving away the shooter's position. Trent noted the shooter's body composition.

Tall, lanky. Michaels.

Trent pivoted, took a deep breath, and raised his weapon. Then held his breath and fired, aiming for center mass. He exhaled and watched as Michaels staggered backward, then returned fire.

He's wearing a vest.

"Kevlar!" Trent called to Olivia, who nodded without turning.

Jake pulled Chelsea into the trees to Trent's left and whispered to her. She nodded and took off running in a zig-zag pattern. Jake removed his Sig Sauer from its holster and crept toward Trent.

"Is it just the one?"

"So far. It's Michaels. Where's Chelsea going?"

"Your terrible plan is slightly less terrible given the circumstances. I told her exactly where to go to draw the Marines out from Camp David."

"And you know this how?"

Jake grinned and whispered, "I've flown out here once or twice with the big guy."

"Way to hold out on your team, West."

"I would've told you eventually."

"Why isn't Michaels shooting?"

"I don't know. I'm more worried about where Martin is. He's a tech guy, but he's been through basic training. He'll know how to fire a weapon."

Olivia jerked her head sharply toward the tall, scraggly Japanese stiltgrass dotting the side of the hill. She turned toward Trent and Jake and pointed to the stand of high grass then put a finger to her lips. Trent's heart pounded as she crept toward the hill in a crouch.

She peered down and then raised one finger in the air. She walked to the far edge of the ridge and fired a warning shot into it. A muffled curse sounded from within the scrubby clump of weeds. She dove into the brush.

"What's she doing?" Jake groused.

"Kicking ass and taking names—Martin's, I suspect. Cover me." Trent sprinted toward the kerfuffle, which Olivia currently seemed to be winning.

When Trent slid down the hill, he found Olivia sitting on Craig Martin's back with her gun pressed against his temple.

"Can you take care of it from here?" she asked, getting to her feet.

In answer, Trent dragged Craig Martin to his feet and pushed him toward the edge of the rock.

"Hey, Michaels, come get your boy," he shouted.

Martin spat into the dirt at Trent's feet. Trent cuffed him in the side of the head.

"That's rude."

Michaels was pressed against the side of the cabin.

"I think he's out of ammo," Olivia called to Jake. "Watch to see if he reloads."

Michaels did appear to be out of ammunition. But instead of reloading, he tossed the rifle aside and took off running, arms and legs pumping. Jake fired into the ground at Michaels' feet. Jake kept firing, and Michaels kept running.

When Trent realized what Jake was doing, he snorted with laughter. Jake was herding Michaels straight into the path of four assault-rifle-toting Marines who were running toward the cabin with Chelsea bringing up the rear.

16

Ten days later

They held the party at Leilah Khan's garage, which would've been weird except that Leilah's garage was smack in the middle of a private racing club that rivaled any ritzy country club for poshness and her bevy of gleaming exotic cars lived in nicer accommodations than did any of the humans in attendance—Leilah included. The row of bedroom suites that lined the garage's loft was yet another benefit of the location. They could celebrate and then crash in the apartments.

Omar uncorked a bottle of Champagne with a refined *pop* and filled the line of glasses. Marielle passed out the flutes and urged everyone to take a perfect pastel macaron as well.

Olivia nibbled the cookie. "You finally found a *pâtisserie* that makes these to your standards?"

Marielle laughed a tinkling laugh and pushed her glasses up on her nose. "No, actually Omar made them."

Leilah turned in slow motion, her jaw dropping. "He did not."

"He did, I swear!"

Omar shrugged. "Guilty as charged. Elle mentioned liking them when we were in D.C. that day. She wished we could detour to this pastry shop in Georgetown that makes *okay* but not great macarons. I didn't even know what they were, but I figured, how hard could they be?"

Olivia raised an eyebrow and took another nibble. "I'm impressed."

"I'm suspicious," Leilah countered. "He probably found a French chef to make them for him."

"I didn't, sis. I'm a man of many talents."

Leilah pursed her lips. "Anyway, moving on from Omar's *alleged* talents, let's toast to Ryan's *actual* victory. To Ryan, who secured indictments against one CIA director, one U.S. Marshal, Jillian and Craig Martin, and a whole mess of senators."

They raised their glasses. "To Ryan."

He took a sip of champagne, then said, "Seriously, this was a team effort. And what a team. From Leilah's precision driving to evade Cumberland's goons to Marielle and Omar's crack research and Chelsea and Jake's human tracking skills, everyone played their part to perfection."

"Ahem," Trent fake-coughed.

"Oh, right, and who could forget Trent and Olivia, without whom none of us would have been in this mess in the first place?" Ryan cracked.

Olivia rolled her eyes and drank her sparkling wine.

Trent leaned over. "He gives me too much credit. We both know we got into the mess pretty much entirely thanks to you."

"You're too kind."

Ryan made his way over to their corner of the garage. "You know I'm only kidding, right?"

"We know," Olivia assured him. "But do you think any of these people will go to jail? I mean

Martin and Michaels, sure, but they were just doing the grunt work."

Ryan leveled his gaze on hers. "I assure you that *a lot* of very important people will spend *a lot* of time in the federal prison system thanks to you and Trent."

Trent wrapped an arm around Ryan's shoulder. "And we know we can count on you to get those convictions, Mr. Prosecutor."

"About that—" Ryan shot Jake a look.

Olivia wrinkled her forehead at Trent, who shrugged.

Jake, who'd been losing badly at darts to Chelsea, cleared his throat. "This is a dual-purpose party. Potomac has made some new hires that I'm especially proud of."

Everyone was shooting everyone else confused glances.

Jake held up a hand and started ticking off his fingers. "First, Ryan's coming aboard as our general counsel."

"You are?" Leilah asked.

"Yeah. This thing soured me on the political side of the Justice Department. Instead of pursuing the case, they tried to kill it. I'd rather work for Jake, who I know will act in the interests of justice."

"Cool," Trent said. "Glad to have you aboard."

"I can't believe it, buddy!" Omar enthused.

"Which brings me to my second new hire. Omar's grown tired of staking out empty warehouses and pretending to be a drug addict, so he'll be bringing his considerable skill set to the security and investigation side of Potomac."

"Sweet!"

"Hang on, I'm not finished. Marielle is joining us as Chief Digital Analyst and Virtual Investigator *and* Olivia is coming aboard to work with Trent and Omar."

"*If* you can confirm that there's no prohibition against fraternization," Olivia reminded Jake.

"You can keep dating Trent, but, as Chelsea would say, do us all a favor and get a room."

Through the peals of laughter, Marielle called to Olivia, "I'm so happy we'll be working together again."

"Me, too! And I'm happy you're getting out of that viper's nest."

The Agency was in disarray after Cumberland's arrest, and more than a few analysts blamed Elle for her part in it.

"But that coworker dating thing, that applies to everyone, not just you and Trent, right?" Elle whispered.

Olivia cocked her head. "I think so. Why?"

"No reason."

"Huh."

Leilah elbowed Chelsea. "I don't know about you, but I'm feeling left out."

"Not me," Chelsea said, wide-eyed. "I don't ever need to be shot at again."

"Okay, that's a solid point. Oh, you need more champagne." She refilled Chelsea's glass and shot Trent a meaningful look. "Anybody else need a refill? Omar, open another bottle."

"What's that all about?" Olivia asked Trent, as Leilah pushed fresh flutes into people's hands.

Trent cleared his throat. "Well, this is a multi-multipurpose party. We're celebrating Ryan's victory, Jake's hiring frenzy, and ... close your eyes."

She stared at him. He stared back at her, unusually serious and unsmiling. Scared even. Although her stomach twisted, she did as he asked. She heard whispering and then a soft thud at her feet.

"Okay, open them and look down."

She opened her eyes to see a domed wooden chest with intricate curlicues carved into the sides sitting on the floor in front of her. She looked up at Trent.

"Is that—that's my grandmother's hope chest?"

"It is. Open it up?"

Her heart leapt into her throat as she slowly undid the latch, raised the lid, and stared down at the thin, rectangular chestnut tray that was set into the right side of the box. In the tray was the white lace ring pillow from her grandparents' wedding, yellowed with age. And on the pillow sat a gold ring with a big, fat, brilliant blue sapphire in the center of it.

She shook her head. "I don't understand."

Trent plucked the ring from the pillow and lowered himself to one knee. "I told you that day in the cabin that your ex-husband was wrong. There's nothing I want more than to go through life as your partner, if you'll have me. You're smart, strong, compassionate, challenging, and fearless. And you have the most unbelievably beautiful blue eyes I've ever seen. They're the exact color of this stone. When I saw it, I knew this ring was meant for you. I know this is fast, really fast, but I'm sure about it. Olivia, will you marry me?"

She stared at the ring in Trent's hand. She couldn't think. She couldn't speak. She assumed she must be breathing.

Finally, Marielle said, "Olivia, say something. The champagne's going to lose its fizz while you make up your mind."

That snapped her out of it. "No."

"No?" Trent repeated.

"No, not *no*. No, I'm not trying to make up my mind. I know. I just ... I can't believe it."

He grimaced. "Is that a ... yes?"

"Yes! Yes, it's a yes!"

"Took her long enough," Chelsea said out of the side of her mouth.

"Eh, it was fun watching Trent sweat," Jake said.

Trent got to his feet and took Olivia's hand in his. He slipped the ring onto her finger, and the unfamiliar weight of it drove home that this was real. It was really happening.

As their friends raised their glasses, Olivia

stepped forward and cupped Trent's face in her hands. "I'm sorry it took so long to respond. You surprised me."

"That's okay. You surprise me every day."

He drew her close and covered her mouth with his. She tasted champagne bubbles and sugary cookies and Trent. She threw her arms around his neck and leaned in, hungrily, for more.

"Get. A. Room," Chelsea shouted.

"Great idea," she retorted.

Then she pulled Trent by the hand up the stairs to the loft apartments.

ABOUT THE AUTHOR

USA Today bestselling author Melissa F. Miller was born in Pittsburgh, Pennsylvania. Although life and love led her to Philadelphia, Baltimore, Washington, D.C., and, ultimately, South Central Pennsylvania, she secretly still considers Pittsburgh home.

In college, she majored in English literature with concentrations in creative writing poetry and medieval literature and was stunned, upon graduation, to learn that there's not exactly a job market for such a degree. After working as an editor for several years, she returned to school to earn a law degree. She was that annoying girl who loved class and always raised her hand. She practiced law for fifteen years, including a stint as a clerk for a federal judge, nearly a decade as an attorney at major international law firms, and several years running a two-person law firm with her lawyer husband.

Now, powered by coffee, she writes legal thrillers and homeschools her three children. When she's not writing, and sometimes when she is, Melissa travels around the country in an RV with her husband, her kids, and her dog and cat.

Connect with me:
www.melissafmiller.com

CPSIA information can be obtained
at www.ICGtesting.com
Printed in the USA
LVHW030058030323
740777LV00004B/437